MOTHER
LOVED
FUNERALS

Roland Curram

MOTHER
LOVED
FUNERALS

Times in the life of
Billy Bartlett

Matador
5 Weir Road
Kibworth Beauchamp, LE8 0LQ
Tel: (+44) 116 2792299

Email: books@troubador.co.uk
Web: www.troubador.co.uk/matador

ISBN: 9781848762701

Typeset in 11pt StempleGarramond by Troubador Publishing Ltd, Leicester, UK

Matador is an imprint of Troubador Publishing Ltd

Printed in Great Britain by the MPG Books Group, Bodmin and King's Lynn

For Kay

Acknowledgements

I owe a great debt of gratitude to Jan Waters for her advice, counsel and encouragement while I was writing this story. To Paul Linn thanks are due for his generous assistance and enthusiasm for the project, and particularly for taking the photograph on the front and back of the cover. Thanks are also due to the inestimable Jeremy Thompson and all at Matador publishing for their help.

*When I was younger I could remember anything, whether
it had happened or not.*
Mark Twain (1835–1910)

*Nothing fixes a thing so intensely in the memory
as the wish to forget it.*
Michel de Montaigne (1533–1592)

*That dark and secret river, full of strange time,
forever flowing past us to the sea.*
Thomas Wolfe (1900–1938)

Contents

Characters

Billy Bartlett – the actor
Annie Bartlett – his actress wife
Violet Phyllis – Billy's mother
Joe – Violet's third husband
Stan – Violet's second husband
Bernard Bartlett – Billy's father
Ralph Bartlett – Billy's uncle
Stella, Pop-Goes-Your-Heart – Ralph's wife
Charlie – Billy's architect friend
Rebecca Bartlett – Billy's daughter
James Bartlett – Billy's son
Norman Marshall – the theatrical director
Peggy Guggenheim – the art connoisseur
Giovanni – a gondolier
Evelyn – Violet's elder sister
Aunt Alice – Violet and Evelyn's aunt
Richard Malleson – a retired managing director
Sandy Lane – a pop singer
Dr Ferris – Violet's doctor
Richard Davies – Violet's solicitor

Part One

Chapter One

Joe's Call

1976

"It's about your Mother!" hissed Annie, holding out the phone with an 'Oh my God!' expression.

Oh, no, I thought, my heart plummeting.

Mother has been the bane of my life; I've wanted to throttle her since I was eight years old. We'd not spoken for nearly ten years. For the last two years I'd been appearing twice weekly in a television soap opera, so it's possible she may have seen me, but I wasn't banking on it. What's up? I wondered. Is she ill, dying? Have the tabloids traced her and been bothering her? Maybe – God forbid – she'd given them a story, 'My Ungrateful Son.' I took the receiver.

"Hello," I said brightly, trying to disguise my foreboding.

It wasn't actually her, thank heaven; it was her ancient third husband, Joe Walsh. Sounding somewhat wheezy he said, "Billy, my dear fellow! How are you? I'll come straight to the point. Your mother doesn't know I'm calling, but could you possibly go and see her? It would be grand if you could manage to."

"What's the matter, Joe? Is everything okay?" I asked. "How is she?"

"Oh, she's fine. It's me who's in the wars, I'm afraid. Fell out of a tree and hurt me back. I'm in hospital as a matter of fact. So she's all alone. Could you go down, at all? Take care of her for while? There's no one else I can ask. Her sister's none too well either."

"How on earth did you manage to fall out of a tree, Joe? What were you doing up it?"

"I was trimming it for your mother. The top was casting a shadow over the sink and she asked me to lop it off. So I did. Lopped meself off, too!"

"Joe! What are you like? Look, I'm pretty busy at the moment," I lied, "I couldn't possibly manage anything till next month...."

Annie raised her eyebrows. "Go," she mouthed, waving her fingers at me.

Hesitantly I continued, "But, um, I do have a break due, maybe I could move it forward..."

"That would be so grand, Billy. I know she'd love to see you. It would mean a lot. Can't go on like this forever, you know. I'll let her know you're on your way. Do you have a pencil? Take this telephone number."

I wrote down his hospital number, said goodbye and took a deep breath. After all this time had I actually said I'd go? I looked at Annie. "He wants me to go and stay with her."

"Great!" said my wife, her green eyes laughing at me. "How long will you be gone?"

"No. I can't go."

"Dar-ling," she reprimanded. "You've been wanting closure with the wretched woman for years, for God's sake, go. It's the perfect opportunity. You'll have to see her one day, face it."

She was right, of course, she usually was. I bit my lip and nodded.

"Just forgive her." She put her hands on either side of my shoulders and gave me a kiss, "Yourself, too." Annie knew me well, we'd been married for over fourteen years, her sunny presence a constant delight; she knew as well as I did that my relationship with my mother had become, well, cumbersome, shall we say? Painful, fearful, and yes, funny, too, in a way, which at least stopped me hating the sight of her, for unintentionally, she did make me laugh.

Over the years I seem to have become captive of some neurotic anxiety about her. Did she actually do those wicked things I remember, or did I imagine it? Oh, I know people say the past is over and finished with but, well, no actually, it's not finished with, that's the problem. It's not finished with at all. My dread of her has become a bit of an emotional dilemma for me, a kind of forbidden territory.

That night, lying beside my beautiful Annie, memories, like angry wasps stirred from their nest by Joe's phone call, stung the inside of my brain. Those painful forbidden memories returned, yanking that damned umbilical cord deep inside my psyche. Perversely I found myself obligated to sift through the ashes of those childhood recollections. Brooding over what happened on that particular day, that day so many years ago when the scales dropped from my eyes. That moment I've tried so hard to forget all my life. It becomes like picking a scab, or what Mark Twain called 'swallowing the frog', meaning dealing with The Big Problem. I never dealt with it up to now. Oh, I kidded myself I had by refusing to see her, but now I've agreed to visit her, be reconciled, now she's an old lady, I suppose I really should try, then live on through, be free of her. If only I could.

Chapter Two

A Fallen Star

1937

Mother loved funerals. I'm told that in the undertaker trade, such characters are not uncommon and are known as 'coffin chasers'. Like a tigress hunting her prey, or in Mother's case, a diva chasing melodramas, she'd travel miles to attend a burial or cremation, an entombment, last rite, obsequy, requiem, or solemnity that would offer her the opportunity of unleashing an Oscar-worthy display of mortification.

Violet Phyllis had charm in bucket-loads – when she wanted to, indeed she was adored as a divinity by many of those around her. She dressed impeccably, and was exceptionally beautiful, rather in the manner of the old movie star Joan Crawford to whom she bore an uncanny likeness. A likeness she was exceedingly proud of, and emphasised by adopting similar hairstyles and fashions, styles that altered along with Miss Crawford's persona over the years, trans-forming her from bug-eyed flapper in the twenties to grande dame drama queen in the eighties and nineties. As a boy I absolutely worshiped her. Mother, that is. I quite liked Joan Crawford, too, but that was because Mother did.

The trouble was that Mother was not a movie star but, to her eternal frustration, a very ordinary, commonplace housewife. Like a 20th century Madame Bovary, she constantly yearned to escape the banalities and emptiness of her provincial life, longing for glamour, to be the centre of attention, and to be loved by every man she met.

Nowhere was this more apparent to me, as a boy, than at a funeral. I thought her quite bewitching, watching her grieve by a graveside. Wearing one of her own millinery creations, with a sooty blobbed veil seductively masking her eyes, a tailored suit in flattering black, elegant patent leather high heels, clutching a matching patent leather handbag and a flower in her gloved hand, she conquered grief magnificently. With mascaraed eyelashes downcast and scarlet lips slightly parted, she clung bravely to the arm of a relative or friend, until that inevitable moment (her timing was flawless), when it all became too much, and we were treated to the long-awaited impassioned crack-up, a display wondrous to behold. Normality would be resumed at the wake after a plethora of sympathy and a large gin and tonic.

I have an indelible memory of her taking me to a funeral in Ruislip when I was a little boy. It was pouring with rain and the departed was Mother's brother, Cecil. After the ushers had moved away, rolling up the canvas webs with which they'd lowered the coffin, Mother moved forward, taking me, who was holding her hand, with her. It was the first time I'd ever looked down into an open grave and I suppose I was a bit scared, for I pulled away. Mother let go my hand and took another step forward. What with the rain, those high heels, the muddy floorboards we were standing on, and of course, her crippling grief, she lost her footing.

The world froze as I watched her fall. Down, down she went, tumbling as if in slow motion. Helpless, we mourners stood by breathless. With limbs outstretched, her hands trying to grasp the sides, she slithered down; those tight kid gloves of hers unable to grip the muddy walls... powerless, she just slid, until, with a loud thump, she landed on the coffin lid. For a moment everyone stared in astonished silence, then all hell broke loose. There were shrieks of humiliation from Mother, screams and gasps of astonishment from the watching ladies, and consternation all around. There she sat on top of the coffin in all her finery at the bottom of the grave. The rain poured down, her hat was skew-whiff, the beautiful suit mud-smeared, her shoe was missing and she was bereft of all dignity, but what an effect. A fallen star!

Amid the "Ohs" and "Ahs", the men folk attempted to reach down to pull her out, but without kneeling and getting their best suits dirty, they didn't have much success. Some of the mourners, with a more alert sense of the ridiculous, started giggling. I was riveted. How on earth, I thought, are we going to get her out? Bystanders and chauffeurs from the waiting cars attracted by the screams, hurried over with their umbrellas, even the gravediggers, standing a little way off, arrived with their shovels. For one ghastly moment I thought they'd arrived to fill in the grave, but at the surreal sight of Mother, an uncomfortably wet, well-dressed lady in black sitting on the coffin putting on her high-heeled shoe, they downed spades and knelt to help her out – they weren't averse to getting their trousers dirty. Down and over they stretched to grasp her hand, but Mother was only five feet tall, and even in high heels (I can still hear the sound they made on the coffin), her fingertips only just touched the gravedigger's. He almost succeeded – with his mate holding onto his legs – in grasping her, but Mother could see that her suit was going to get even dirtier against the muddy wall if she did it his way.

"Haven't you got a ladder?" she called up crossly. She wanted it done her way.

Ushers conferred with the gravediggers and someone was dispatched. While we waited, gentlemen held their umbrellas up over the grave, and people called down, "Are you alright down there, Violet?" It was a truly macabre sight. I suppose Mother must have noticed my distressed expression for she waved and blew me a kiss, calling, "Don't worry, Precious. I'll be fine."

Someone asked if she'd like a cigarette, but she shook her head in exasperation. I had a toffee in my pocket and considered throwing it down to her, but I didn't.

Eventually, a ladder was produced and carefully lowered.

So commenced her grand exit, or entrance, whichever way you looked at it. She retrieved her handbag, straightened her suit into the correct position, adjusted her hat and veil, and then, and only then, did she consent to mount. Up she came, scuffed, muddied and bruised, but with her head held as high as if she was the Duchess of Windsor herself. Reaching ground level, there were congratulations, sympathy, and even light applause. Gradually everyone made their way to the waiting cars and the reception, Mother surrounded by gentlemen admirers, my deceased Uncle Cecil totally forgotten.

After the reception, as we left, I overheard someone say, "Wasn't Vi wonderful?" as if they were coming out of a theatre. And, of course, there you have it. She really should have been an actress; she might have done very well, she certainly had the flair. That particular experience didn't seem to put her off funerals, for I remember several others when she didn't fall in the grave, but when she always gave a jolly good show. She loved 'em. A funeral, to her, seemed to be a theatre where she could perform and take centre stage. She'd never admit that, of course. In fact she went to great lengths to make known the fact she didn't attend funerals. But you try and keep her away! The point being, that when she was finally persuaded to appear, her presence was even more valued, and the consequent drama she produced more effective and affecting.

Well, that's the thing about funerals, they're primed emotional platforms. I've noticed lately there's a tendency in some circles for lamentations of grief to become histrionic performances, as an actor I'm particularly aware of that. When the time comes to speak at Mother's funeral I'll ask the vicar, but she'll probably outlive me, for she belongs to that determined breed of English women who survive wars, husbands, hip and knee replacements, and still manage to bend everyone to their will – everyone that is, except my Father's.

Chapter Three

Call him Daddy

1937

I only have the faintest memory of my father, and none at all of us all living together as a family. I spent most of my childhood imagining him, listening for his voice, wondering what he'd make of me; in a sense he became my conscience when I was a young man. Would Father approve of that? Can Father see me doing this?

There's a snap of me somewhere as an infant sitting cross-legged on a lawn wearing woollen shorts in front of a birthday cake with four candles on it; in the background is a long institutional building with the words "Ventnor Children's Home" clearly visible. Fortunately I have no memory of that time either, but I've often wondered why I was there.

I have a persistent memory of staying in a foster home where a woman sat me on her lap and asked, "Who do you love best, me or the mother who has deserted you?"

When I answered "Mother", she hit me with a stick.

As a child, an only child, I had not a notion of what my mother was really about. To me, she was then an adored angel, how could she possibly be anything else? When the thing happened, I knew it was wrong and wicked, but her outwardly loving behaviour deceived me as it did everyone else. As I think about it now though, so many years after the event, I'm shocked by my naivety, for there were clear warnings beforehand that crucial truths were being kept from me, and things were not as rosy as I imagined.

One sunny afternoon in 1937 I was putting up my little orange tent in the garden of the bungalow we lived in at Selsey Bill in Sussex – according to the black and white snaps in Mother's photograph album, I looked like any other middle-class seven-year-old with a mop of brown hair, wearing shorts and a short-sleeved Aertex shirt. Mother's gentleman friend, a boring man she'd asked me to call 'Uncle' Stan, who was always listening to the news about Herr Hitler on the wireless, was mowing the lawn in his braces. I was kneeling on an area he'd already cut intent on pushing a meat skewer into the earth to hold down the tent. Mother, wearing a dazzling floral summer dress, came out of the French windows with a tray of tea things. "Billy, darling!" she announced. "Stan and I have something to tell you." Smiling radiantly, she set down the tray and casually dropped the bomb. "From today onwards we've decided you should call him 'Daddy'."

I remember thinking that was a bit odd. "But what about Daddy?" I answered. Although I'd not seen my father for ages I knew he was around somewhere; one of my most valued possessions was his hairbrush, though I seldom brushed my hair, when I did, his brush was always the one I used. I'd combed out all his hairs from it and put them in a little ornamental snuff box.

"I can't have two Daddies."

"Well," she added, drawing up a deck chair and preparing to pour the tea, "maybe you could call Stan, 'Pop'? That would be rather nice, wouldn't it?"

"I don't think it would," I came back with. "It sounds like a ginger beer bottle going off!"

"Does it?" she said, her smile freezing. "Well, I think it sounds rather aristocratic. Anyway, he's won't answer you unless you do, so there."

So I did. I recall writing, rather shamefacedly, one or two letters to him from my preparatory boarding school addressing him as

'Dear Pop'. I suppose I wanted him to like me. I wanted to write to my real Daddy too, all about the rabbits and guinea pigs I was keeping at school, but I had no address for him. Nobody appeared to know where he was, or if they did, they never told me. Even when I sent him a Christmas card, Mother had addressed the envelope and posted it.

It was not until many years later I came to fully understand why recollections of my father were so hazy. It was when his brother, my Uncle Ralph, told me the following story about him.

Chapter Four

Ralph's Story

1961

"When Bernard left your mother," said Uncle Ralph, sipping his brandy, "you were abandoned in the turmoil." Catching my eye, he added, "Sadly," and the tanned crow's feet around his eyes crinkled up into a smile.

My Uncle Ralph was an ex naval Lieutenant Commander and we'd just finished Sunday lunch in his comfortably furnished bungalow at Worthing where he'd retired. I was thirty-one at the time and had recently married. Ralph had been unable to attend our wedding at Stratford upon Avon, so after our honeymoon, I'd driven Annie, my new young bride, down from London to show her off. She had just cleared away the dishes with Uncle's wife, my aunt Stella, and together they'd retired to the kitchen. Aunt Stella was a keen W.V.S. member; a tall, pretty woman who always wore a long bugle-bead necklace that dangled down her flat chest to her tummy. Uncle's nick-name for her was 'Pop-Goes-Your-Heart', presumably because that's the effect she had on him, so that, in turn, became my name for her, too: Auntie Pop-Goes-Your-Heart. Anyway, while she and Annie were in the kitchen, Uncle and I were alone, and, as always when we were alone, I pumped him for stories about my mysterious Father. Mother never mentioned him, and, for reasons that will become clear, I never asked her about him. I knew only that he'd been the cause of some deep unhappiness. There were no photographs of him anywhere in

Mother's house, whereas here, on Uncle's sideboard, there were several. My favourite was a beach scene taken when he was a teenager, my Dad wore nothing but a swimming costume and he and Ralph were sanding proudly arm in arm astride an elaborate sandcastle they'd built, their older sister, Gertie, wearing a big floppy straw hat, was looking on grinning. Whenever Uncle Ralph spoke of my father I devoured his every syllable.

"I can assure you he felt very bad about it, too... leaving you," Uncle continued, rising from the dining table and making for the number one armchair in the front living-room area. Ralph sailed a yacht he owned jointly with his mates in the Solent every week, which accounted for his weather-beaten features, his merry disposition accounted for his Father Christmas-like cheeks and the laugh lines round his eyes. "After the divorce, though, your mother got custody. So what could he do? He virtually cast you off, too." Uncle sat in his high-backed chair, set his brandy glass on the side table, reached for his pipe and started filling it. "You didn't fit in with his plans, y'see. He had some lassie in tow. What was her name, now? Linda! That's it."

"I remember Auntie Linda," I cried, joining him by the fireplace. "Pretty, blonde woman, she used to sign my leave-out pass on Sundays when I was at school."

"I daresay. She was a chum of your mother's. They'd owned that hat shop in Hove together."

"Philinda's!" I exclaimed. I'd always known Mother had been a milliner and had run a hat shop. One of my earliest memories was of her workroom with wooden hat blocks on shelves, felt hoods on a big white table and pins on the floor. At her home, among her sewing things, there were still rolls of ribbon embroidered with 'Philinda Excusive Millinery 177a, Church Road Hove' for the lining of hats. "Mother told me she'd combined her middle name, Phyllis, with Linda's, to come up with the name of their shop; she said if she'd used 'Violet', it would have sounded like a music shop, 'Violinda'."

"Well, your Dad went off with her."

"No!" I'd never been told anything about that. I'd been quite unaware that my father had left my Mother for her best friend, and the tragic effect that must have had on her. As I digested this, Uncle struck a match and lit his pipe.

"Mind you," he said dryly as he puffed, "she didn't last long. He actually got engaged to some other woman."

"What other woman?" I asked.

"Well, hardly a woman, a girl more like, pretty little thing. Winifred was her name, a hairdresser, nurse, or some such, I think she was."

"Did they get married? Don't tell me I have a step-mother somewhere?"

"You might have had," said Uncle, looking at me roguishly as he held the lighted match, "if your mother hadn't have turned up at the wedding." He blew the flame out with perfect timing and deposited the match in the ashtray.

"What?" I cried. All ears I perched excitedly on the chair opposite him. "Mother turned up at Father's second wedding? Where? Tell me. What happened?"

"Proper lark, that all was." Sucking his pipe he grinned at the memory and his crow's feet crinkled up again. "This was in, oh, '38 or so, before the war, just before the Munich crisis. I was your father's Best Man, all spiffed-up in my Dress kit, I was." As uncle talked, I glanced at the photograph of him on the mantelshelf dressed in full naval officer's dress regalia with sword up. The picture had been taken outside Buckingham Palace when he'd been given his D.S.O. He looked magnificently upright, young and noble. "We were staying at The Branksome Towers Hotel in Bournemouth," he was saying. "We'd assembled in the foyer to go off to the Registry office. Pop-Goes-Your-Heart was all done-up in her beads. Your Dad was in his best blue suit, flower in his buttonhole and all. Very natty dresser, your Dad. Handsome lad, too, well, he was only twenty-nine at the time. Girls went potty about him. Of course, it was the second time round for him, so he was a tad nervous, understandably. So there we all are in the entrance hall, with your potted palms and your Max Jaffa quartet playing 'Merry England', kicking our heels at the bottom of the stairs waiting for the young bride. She appears at the top of the stairs. Slowly, down she comes looking just dandy, dolled-up in some yellow drifty thing. Lovely girl, she was, fluffy blonde type. So we're all set. Well, we're just about to leave, when through the revolving doors comes y'mother, breathing fire, in her wake, your stepfather, Stan. Well, you can imagine. Pole axed, we were, I mean none of us has clapped eyes on her for years. Not since y'father and she had been divorced. We'd heard she'd had some sort of breakdown, but in she breezes all guns blazing. Ignores us, goes straight up to your Dad and grabs him. 'You've not done it, have you?'

'Done what?' he says.

'Got married?' she says.

'No,' he answers, all wary.

'Thank God I'm in time,' she says. 'Now why are you doing this? Best come home with me, Bernard. You don't have to be doing this thing.'

"Thing', mind, she says, 'thing!' Well, young Winfred grabs his other arm double quick. 'Bernie,' she says, 'who is this woman?'

"This is my ex-wife," he says, a bit sheepish. 'Violet.'

"Tell her to go away," says Winifred.

'You heard her,' he says to Vi. 'Leave us be. We're going to be married.'

'Oh no, you're not!' says Vi. 'You're coming home with Stan

17

and me,' and she starts pulling him to the door. 'Come along, now, you're not well. I know all about it. Your sister, Gertie, told me. You'll never have to go to another sanatorium as long as you're with me, I promise you that. I'll nurse you. Come on, it's me you love really, you know you do.'

"All this time young Winifred is clinging on to your Dad on his other side. And then what? Those two girls, they start having a tug-of-war with him. Calling out and cursing each other, they are. Right there in the foyer of The Branksome Towers Hotel with all the guests looking on. Oh, dreadful, it was, most embarrassing."

That my conservative uncle should be embarrassed by Mother's behaviour in public did not surprise me. Grinning I asked, "Didn't you do anything?"

"I knew better than to interfere with your father and his women. No, no. Pop-Goes-Your-Heart and I just stood by waiting, hoping it would all end double quick. Then your stepfather, Stan, joins in. He was an old friend of your Dad's. They'd been in The Liverpool and Victoria Insurance together. In fact, I think it was your father that actually introduced him to your mother. Anyway, he goes round the other side to where young Winifred is hanging on. 'Come along now, Bernard, old chap,' he says, disentangling the girl. 'You come home with Vi and me. We'll look after you. That'll be best. Be a good chap, now.'

"And what do you think? Bernard trots along after them! Leaves his young bride flat and goes. Well, we were amazed, you can imagine. Pop-Goes-Your-Heart couldn't believe it. Open-mouthed, we were. Young Winifred's calling after him, 'Bernie! Bernie! Come back.' But he ignores her. No, that's not quite true. Actually, he called over his shoulder that he'd write her a letter. Don't know whether he did or not. Your mother and Stan just frog-marched him out. Straight through the main exit doors and down the steps into the back of Stan's Morris Minor parked outside. And off they all drive to Addington, or wherever it was they were living. Hardly put up any struggle at all, he did; well, he didn't, not at all. No suitcase, nothing. Beats me why he went. Still does to this day. Imagine it, dumping a pretty little thing like Winifred on your wedding day, in favour of a termagant like your mama. It's not as if he didn't know what he was getting into. Well, I don't have to tell you about her. To tell you the truth, old boy, I never thought he had all that much feeling for her... your mother, I mean, even when they were married. Oh, she was good looker, I grant her that, but she was always a bit of a... well, you know what Pop-Goes-Your-Heart thinks of her."

I nodded as if I did. Actually I didn't, but I could guess. Mother's opinion of my Auntie Pop-Goes-Your-Heart echoed in my ears. "Selfish bloody woman. She's never given birth. Only thinks of herself and that breezy husband of hers."

Uncle sat puffing his pipe wrapped in thought. "He was my young brother and I loved him dearly, but I'm afraid your dear Dad didn't have much of a back bone, and your mother, as we all know, is a very strong woman. She had some hold over him. I could never fathom it myself. I've often wondered what it was."

I didn't have to think too hard to answer that. Not that I did answer him, of course, for that would have meant swallowing the frog.

Chapter Five

Under the Bed

1938

When Father came back to live with us at our new home in Addington, I was away at boarding school, so the whole ménage-a-trois thing didn't impinge on me till much later.

It was around the time of the so-called Phoney war, when Britain was on the brink of war. In September 1938, Neville Chamberlain, the Prime Minister, met Adolph Hitler at his home in Berchtesgaden; Hitler had threatened to invade Czechoslovakia unless Britain supported Germany's plans to take over the Sudetenland; Chamberlain told Hitler that his proposals were unacceptable.

With war looming, the Government agreed that the mass evacuation of children, mothers of small children, pregnant women, invalids, and the elderly would have to be carried out from cities to places of safety. Some 1,500,000 people took up the offer, and my school was among them. We were all due to be bundled into coaches and trains with our gas masks, regulation clothing and toothbrushes, tagged like pieces of luggage, and sent off to mysterious destinations. Early, on the morning of our departure, I remember we took part in a fire practice drill; we all slid down an improvised ramp from our top floor dormitory. I thought it enormous fun.

I know now it was an historic day for the world, and certainly, as it turned out, it was for me. The 30th of September 1938, when the four-power meeting, consisting of Hitler, Mussolini, Edouard Daladier and Neville Chamberlain, signed the Munich agreement which transferred Sudetenland to Germany, in return Hitler promised not to make any more territorial demands. The newspapers showed Chamberlain returning home, waving that silly piece of paper claiming he'd secured 'Peace for our Time', so we didn't have to be evacuated after all. Instead we went to Chessington Zoo, and after lunch I went home.

In those days we didn't have a telephone, so the Headmaster, Mr Bradley, gave me a letter to give to Mother explaining what had happened. Consequently, all of eight years old, alone and labelled up, I made my way over the thirty miles by train and bus to our 1930's semi-detached house at 62, Addington Crescent, near Croydon.

Eagerly, I walked up the road and into our front garden. Ignoring the front door I went straight around to the back, the side entrance. The kitchen door was unlocked – we didn't lock the doors in those days – and in I went. The kitchen was tidy but deserted.

"Hello," I called, moving into the hall. There was no answer, so I went in further, calling again.

I heard a muffed cry from upstairs.

I mounted the stairs, calling again.

"Billy, is that you?" It sounded very much like Daddy's voice coming from the spare room.

"Daddy?" I called.

I opened the bedroom door and there he was lying in bed. I'd not seen him for over two years, and even though it was clear he was unwell, I was thrilled. I've since seen a photograph of a handsome, strong-looking man, with thick eyebrows like mine, wavy dark hair and a generous mouth. Whenever I was told I looked like him I was very proud, it contradicted my mirror, which told me that, at eight years old, I had a fringe, freckles and a snub nose. This is the one clear memory I have of him, lying in that bed, his lovely smile, the way his hair fell over his forehead and his hairy chest showing through his open blue striped pyjamas. He held out his arms to me and, with a catch in my heart, I flung myself at him.

"My dear Billy boy, what are you doing home?"

I sat on the bed gabbling wildly, telling him of my travels and what had happened at school. He listened to me with one hand on my shoulder and the other stroking my arm. Eventually I asked why he was in bed.

"Not been feeling so hot lately, lad. Been laid up a bit," he answered. "Y'mother's been looking after me. I think she's gone out shopping." There seemed to be an air of sadness about him, as if he was recovering from a lost race.

"Here, look at this," I said, putting on my gas mask and telling him about our fire drill when I'd slid down from our dormitory window.

"I can't hear one word you're saying," he said, laughing. He tried to put the gas mask on himself, but it didn't fit and we laughed some more. I got under his bed and played a game whereby I pushed his mattress up and down by arching my back, which we thought tremendous fun. We were enjoying ourselves hugely when we heard the front door downstairs bang.

"Mummy's back," said Daddy.

I scrambled under the bed again to surprise her.

Daddy quickly passed me my gas mask and school cap and, excitedly, I lay down on my tummy, waiting.

The first thing she said when she came into the room was, "I'm sorry."

I could tell by the way she said it, something was up. I recognised that emotive note in her voice. She closed the bedroom door and stayed there.

"I'm sorry, sorry, sorry," she said again in a rush. "I promise I'll never do that again. Never."

"Forget it," said Daddy.

"But you do make me so mad," she said quietly, still with that tone in her voice. "You always did. You're the only person in the whole world who can do that, you know that? ...the only person who treats me so badly, everyone else..."

"Violet, please...I'm not up to this...not right now..."

"If that's how you felt, why on earth did you agree to come home with me?" She took a step towards us. "Why didn't you say?"

"I told you, because you promised you wouldn't let them take me to another sanatorium. Now let's forget it, please."

"Not because you loved me?"

"Vi," said Daddy. "Not that again, not now."

"You are the only person I've ever loved, Bernard. You know that. You and I were meant to stay together forever. I only ever married Stan because I was lonely. I was at my wits' end when you left me. I could hardly make ends meet, let alone send the boy to that expensive boarding school without Stan. You were no help."

"We've been over this a thousand times. You had the house and the shop..."

"Yes, and you had your bloody fancy woman!"

"Oh, Lord, we're not back to that again!"

"Yes we are, so there. I want this settled here and now. I can't bear it. It's making me ill. Stan will be home soon, and if I'm to take care of you.... and I'm willing to do that, I want to take care of you; you're my whole life.... I don't want that woman's name mentioned, and I want some respect. And I want love."

"Love! I can't love you. I can't love anyone. Look at me, woman, I've hardly got the strength to feed myself. I'm wasting away here."

"It's never stopped you before."

"For God's sake, Vi, leave me alone. This is a business arrangement. I'm paying you rent. That is the agreement I've made with Stan, but I cannot love you. I haven't for a very long time and I never will again. Now stop this, please."

There was silence.

"Did you ever really love me?" Mother asked.

Another silence. She was standing so close to the bed I could have touched her ankles. Wanting to vanish, I held my breath and squirmed even flatter.

"I could kill you when you've got that expression on your face," she murmured.

"Then kill me! At least it'll get it over with. Save us both a lot of suffering. We certainly haven't got much to look forward to this way, have we? Here, take the pillow, do it."

"It would be so easy."

"Then do it. You'll be doing me a favour, believe me."

This is where it gets hazy in my mind. I blocked my ears with my fingers to stop the sound of their voices. The mattress above me lowered as Mother sat down. I flattened myself so much my nose squashed on the carpet and I thought I might sneeze. After what seemed an age, I opened my eyes and unblocked my ears. All I could hear was Mother sobbing. She stood up and ran out of the room.

I stayed stock still not daring to make a sound. After a minute or two I heard the front door downstairs bang. I crawled out from under the bed.

Father lay quite still, his eyes closed; a crumpled pillow beside him.

"Daddy," I whispered.

He didn't move.

Gently I shook him.

Nothing. I studied his face, listening for his breath. Not a sound came from him.

I knew it. He was dead.

I shut my eyes. I saw the pillow smothering his face, his arms trapped by the covers and Mother, her tight fists gripping the pillow fast, holding him down, suffocating the life force out of him... and me only inches away, doing nothing, just letting it happen.

I went to the window and looked out into the street, no sign of her, no one.

What on earth should I do?

Chapter Six

To Tell or not to Tell

1938-1939

No one was around as I closed the garden gate and ran down the road to the bus stop. I caught a train at East Croydon station to take me back to Banstead and school. Sitting in the corner of a deserted carriage looking out of the window at the passing houses and countryside, I had a good long think about what had happened. Should I go to a judge or to a policeman to tell? I thought and thought, and could see no advantage in telling anyone. If I did, my beautiful, sweet-smelling Ma would be taken to the Court and hanged for a killing, then what? I'd be left with boring 'Pop' Stan, or, worse, sent back to the Ventnor Children's Home or to another foster home, and I didn't want that.

It was dark by the time I walked through the school front gate and up the gravel drive. I told Matron I'd come back because my parents were away. She shrugged, said, "What a shame," and gave me some hot soup. There were only three other boys in my dormitory that night, all chattering about what an exciting day they'd had. I held my secret close and never said a word.

And that was the way it stayed, more or less. I locked away what I'd heard, blocked, buried, and forgot it. At least, I tried to. Remembering it, writing this account just now has not been easy, though I confess, it is a kind of relief; it's the first time I've thought about it in such detail since. Though I suspect the scene festered in my unconscious, for, soon afterwards, I started having recurring nightmares.

The school play that Christmas was *The Jolly Tinker*; I played the Tinker and helped paint the scenery. Among the props was a rubber dagger. The blade was painted silver and from a distance it looked most convincing. My dream was that I was stabbing Mother with it, but the real nightmare part of the dream was that the dagger wouldn't go into her, it was all soft and floppy, no matter how many times I stabbed her I wasn't able to kill her.

One doesn't have to be Dr Freud to guess the state of my mind. When Mother came to collect me for the Christmas holidays I was very wary of her.

After breakfast on my first morning home, I was standing by the sink in the kitchen, helping her with the washing up, when she said, "I have something to tell you. While you were away at school, your father died."

I froze. Father's death and Mother's part in it was a festering wound I'd bandaged and blocked. To be faced with the reality of it again unglued my fragile composure. I was unsure how to react. I knew I had to keep secret what I knew. Don't give anything away, I told myself. Slowly I sat down at the table. Feeling wretched, my voice barely under control, I whispered, "How?"

"Tuberculosis. He's been in and out of sanatoriums for years. But finally he, well, he succumbed, I'm afraid."

I looked up into her face. She told me this shameful lie without a flicker of guilt or wrongdoing, but, even at that early age, I realised she was a consummate actress. I cried and she put her arms around me. "Don't cry, Billy. It's not as if you ever knew him well. You've not set eyes on him for years. Do stop, dear. He's not exactly been a good father to you either, admit it, Stan's been more of a Dad to you than ever Bernard was."

At that exact moment a scary sound surprised us. The air-raid siren started whooping and swooping in the frightening way that later became so familiar. 'Wailing Willie' we used to call it, but that was the first time I ever heard it. We only found out later it was a test run.

"The war must have started," said Mother. "The Germans are coming to drop bombs on us! Quick, get to the shelter."

I was terrified. We dashed out into the half-finished Anderson air-raid shelter that Stan had started digging in the garden. I crouched on the mud floor, shivering with fear. Somehow the details of when Daddy's funeral was, why I'd never been told, or even where he was buried, seemed unimportant. Later on, I'm ashamed to admit, I was afraid to ask her.

So there it was... Mother had apparently got away with murder.

Throughout the school holiday I watched her face closely for any sign of guilt, but, apart from shedding a few tears at King George VI's Christmas day speech on the wireless, there was nothing. She was the same as always with me, and with 'Pop' Stan, she carried on their usual routine of lovey-dovey dancing and kissing nonsense.

A battle now took place in my eight-year-old mind. Reassessing my earlier thoughts, my conscience became a minister of war. Should I tell?

Eventually I vocalised some of the misery, rage and acrimony that was swirling around inside my head. My excuse was Mother reprimanding me about my untidy bedroom. "When I'm a grown-up," I answered her, "I'm going to join the R.A.F."

"Are you, dear?" she queried. "Well, that's new!"

"I'm going to get into an airplane and drop a bomb on top of you!"

She didn't laugh. She slapped me round the head saying, "You wicked, wicked child to say something so vile to your mother."

"So are you," I answered, "and you know why!"

She frowned and left the room.

It was soon after that I ran away.

I'd got it into my head that I was going to join the Royal Navy to be a cabin boy and join my Uncle Ralph. He was then stationed at the naval base in Chatham, where I planned to enlist. I guessed that I'd have to lie to the recruiting officer about my age. I remember getting as far as the bus terminus at Croydon where I was stopped by a constable and taken to East Croydon Police Station. He sat me on the counter at the front desk. A posse of policemen gathered around me and asked: "What's your name, sonny? What are you doing out at this time of night? Were you caught in an air raid? Why aren't you tucked up in your bed at home?"

Reluctant to answer, I said nothing. Milk and biscuits were brought; ladies of the night came and went, telephones rang. I'd never been up so late in my life and was rather enjoying myself. The policemen were all friendly but persisted with their questions. Eventually I whispered the truth into the ear of the friendly man with white hair standing behind the counter.

"What was that you said, sonny?" he said. "Speak up."

"My Mummy killed my Daddy."

Whether he heard me or not, I could not tell, for, at that moment in she walked.

She came to collect me wearing a shimmering white evening dress; her hair was in a chignon and she had a white fox fur over her shoulders. She looked just like a film star and the policemen all seemed to fall in love with her. I was so proud of her. How could I ever have thought ill of her? She hugged and kissed me and smelt wonderful. My rebellion was snuffed. She explained she and Stan had been to the theatre to see a Cochran Revue called *Lights Up* (one of the few shows that continued to run during the war) at the Savoy Theatre in London. When they'd returned home they'd discovered I was missing. Frantic with worry, Stan had telephoned the police and had been told I was there. I remember that dress she wore so well. It was made of heavy satin and cut on the cross with a fishtail train. I've since seen Ginger Rodgers wearing something like it in *Top Hat*. Strangely enough, I don't recollect being reprimanded at all as 'Pop' drove us home in his Morris Minor. I do remember wondering if the desk sergeant had heard me and remember what I'd told him. For weeks afterwards I imagined every knock on the front door was the police coming to arrest Mother, telling her I was the one who had given her away.

Chapter Seven

Initiations

1976/1940

It was dark and drizzly as I drove out of Elstree television studios. I'd been on call since 6 a.m. and was exhausted; last night's insomnia caused by reliving life with Mother hadn't helped much either. Alan, the Security guard, called out "'Night, Mr Bartlett," and I waved back, manoeuvring past a band of press photographers and a huddle of loyal fans, most of whom I recognized, who, even in this weather, gathered outside the studio gates. I'd just finished recording my final scene in this week's episode. It had been, wouldn't you know it, a funeral scene, supposedly my daughter's. In reality the actress who played the part had over-stepped the mark with the management by committing the cardinal sin of a soap actor. Over lunch in the studio canteen, where both leading and supporting actors, technicians, producers and directors alike, all ate, she'd stopped by our producer and writer's table to suggest to them what she considered an exciting new storyline for her character. Our lady producer had listened with the impenetrable mask of reserve for which she was famous, but when the actress walked away, had turned to the writer and uttered, with the cutting voice of the executioner, "Write her out!" Consequently 'my daughter' had recently been fatally struck by a truck.

The month's break, which was now my due, was the result of my agent negotiating with the producer three months ago. The writers had obligingly sent my character, 'Old Roly', to Australia to visit his son. Annie and I had intended using the time on re-shaping our garden – we'd planned on laying some decking and planting new shrubs – then taking a ten-day trip to Sorrento, but since Joe's phone call yesterday, our gardening plans would have to go on hold. I had decided, reluctantly, on driving down to Hassocks to see Mother tomorrow, on Saturday morning.

I pushed on through Elstree High Street, passing, as usual, St Nicholas Church with its Norman tower silhouetted against the grey sky. It reminded me, as it always did, of the Norman tower of our old church in Addington where I used to sing in the village choir.

When I was ten years old, Mother decided I should be christened, something to do with the requirements of the new church day school I was to attend. I remember standing by the font in our church announcing, "I want to change my name to Daddy's. I want to be called Bernard."

Mother stood absolutely boiling with fury. She tried to hide her feelings from the vicar, but I knew from the way her eyes nar-rowed and were venomously glaring at me from under her elabo-rately-veiled hat that I'd scored a point. She was livid. I was defi-ant.

My godmother was my father's sister, my jolly Margaret-Rutherford-like Auntie Gertie. "What a splendid notion!" she said. "We could add Bernard as his middle name."

I beamed. Mother had no option but to agree.

I was victorious. Obviously my rebellion was still fermenting. Then something occurred that helped me put all thoughts of Mother's guilt or otherwise out of my head, and concentrated my mind wonderfully on myself... sex.

In the village choir I sang the treble part. In the tenor pew behind me stood a dark haired brawny youth of sixteen or so, called Max. Sometimes we walked home together after choir practice. One sunny evening as we ambled along the lane leading to our respective homes, we passed a newly built haystack. We clambered on top of it, slid down and landed on top of each other; we tussled, fought, and generally romped around. Max was bigger than I was and I remember him sitting on top of me looking deeply into my eyes. I suppose I could claim I was seduced, but that would be untrue, for I was a very willing participant. This was my sexual initiation and I found the encounter tremendous. Max told me I smelt like marzipan and looked like Johnny Sheffield, the boy who played Tarzan's son in the Tarzan films. I didn't dare tell him I thought he looked like Tarzan with his shirt off. Max became my first 'crush', and I thought of him a great deal each night before I fell asleep.

One afternoon soon afterwards I came home from school and found, on the pillow of my bed, a book with a glossy cover. *How a Baby is Born* was a slim volume, and I can still remember 'Johnson's', the people who make baby powder, published it. Mother must have thought – perhaps by the state of my sheets – that I was in need of instruction, but she never mentioned leaving the book there. I skipped swiftly through the first chapters on the birds and the bees, but slowed down when I got to mammals. By the time I reached the last chapter on human beings, I was riveted. I can honestly report that I was astonished. To do that to someone you liked! Wondering what a girl thought about the business and, I suppose, secretly hoping she'd give me a trial run, I showed the book to my friend, Clair Thompson, the girl who lived next door. We were the same age and she did not disappoint me. "Let's try it," she said, her eyes popping. Immediately we set off on our bicycles and pedalled to the nearby woods, where, book in hand, we did what it said. I found it mildly interesting, not as enthralling as what Max and I had done in the haystack, but Clair thought it "absolutely super." What's more, she must have told her friends so. Consequently I became quite popular with some of the girls in my street as I pedalled off with them one by one into the woods, where I managed to instruct them without the help of the book.

During the war, 'Pop' Stan's job was to drive around the countryside in a lorry examining the contents and removing the debris of crashed German aeroplanes that had been shot down. In his and Mother's bedroom, under their double bed he tucked away his spoils: a Lugar revolver and a silk parachute, which, because of clothes rationing, Mother skilfully utilised – she was a wizard with a needle – making it up into underskirts, blouses, shirts and handkerchiefs.

During an air raid one night, 'Wailing Willie' woke us up and we dashed from our beds into the now-completed Anderson shelter in the garden. I must explain that we lived on the side of a hill, with a view of the village below from our kitchen door. Once inside the Anderson shelter, Mother discovered we were short of water, so Stan was dispatched to the kitchen to fetch a pail of water.

By the time he returned she'd discovered we'd run out of sugar. So off he went again. He came back to be told, "Stan, we've no biscuits. Fetch those crumpets I made, too." Yet again he was sent off, this time to boil the kettle and fill the thermos. Returning once more, Mother told him, "Stan, there are no sardines. Fetch some from the cupboard, will you? We might be here all night, tomatoes and vinegar, too. Be careful of the blackout!"

"Yes, dear," he answered, and off he popped again. It was neverending; back and forth, to and fro the poor man went, all at Mother's behest.

After the 'All Clear' sounded, we moved back to our beds in the house for what was left of the night. Rather too soon a knocking on the front door woke us up.

It was three members of the Home Guard, all of whom Stan knew, with bayonets fixed to their rifles. They'd come to arrest him for signalling in Morse code to the German aircraft during the air raid, using the light from the kitchen door.

Off he was marched down the road at bayonet point to the barracks on the hill opposite, from where, they said, they'd observed him signalling. Mother and I stood in our dressing gowns on the front door step watching him being taken away, wondering if we'd ever see him again. The next day more soldiers returned to search the house. When they discovered the parachute and the Lugar under the bed, the game was up. Stan was accused of being a German spy. The Home Guard ordered a trial. I, of course, was not permitted into the courtroom, but that evening over supper, the conversation was about nothing else.

In the witness box Mother had been obliged to confess that the kitchen light had been turned on and off so many times during the air raid because she'd asked Stan to fetch tea and crumpets for the shelter. The Court had erupted into laughter. Mother was furious. "I was so embarrassed," she said, glaring at Stan, "being made a fool of like that in front of everyone. I could cheerfully have throttled you."

That pulled me up. I wondered if she might suffocate him, too.

Apparently Stan's boss was then called into Court and confirmed that his work of clearing away crashed enemy aircraft was not just a simple tidying up job, but by examining them closely and reporting on their contents, his work was of vital importance to our knowledge of the enemy. This explained away the presence of the parachute and the Lugar under the bed, and the case was dismissed. But, thereafter, Stan's reputation was forever sealed as a hen-pecked husband, and Mother's, as a nagging wife.

Perhaps I should have told that story to the writers of *Dad's Army*; they might have turned it into a fun episode. I've often wished Stan really had have been a German spy, it would certainly have made him more interesting to me.

During the school holidays I accompanied Mother to collect, as she called it, 'the bobs and tanners'. She was then working for the Liverpool and Victoria Insurance Company collecting subscriptions from the good citizens of south London. We'd catch an early train from East Croydon to Clapham Junction, or sometimes Battersea, and trudge through the streets of those poor neighbourhoods knocking on the doors of houses and flats collecting the weekly premiums from the householders. Sometimes people couldn't pay up and Mother fed them a lecture. Occasionally we'd be invited in for a cup of tea. Sometimes when we called the following week there'd be nothing but a great hole where the house had stood. There'd be wreckage and pathetic squares of bedroom wallpaper flapping high on the walls of the adjoining house, and the people we'd had tea with had vanished.

As we walked from door to door I remember Mother telling me the most important thing in life was to have money. "Without it, you're a nobody. My mother taught that to me, and I'm teaching it to you now. Remember; no one respects you if you're poor, no one even likes you. You can do nothing in this world unless you have money. It doesn't matter how you acquire it, Billy, just get it. Money is like a force of nature. With it you have freedom to do what you want, without it you're nothing. Work, lie or cheat, and when you've got it, use it wisely."

I had a long think about that. They seemed pretty important sentiments and I wondered how rich my Daddy had been. When she'd made her killing, had she also made a bundle? What had happened in her past to make her feel that way? It took me many years to discover.

After visiting all the addresses in Mother's notebook we'd have a snack lunch and then, wonder of wonders, we'd go for a treat; a visit to the cinema. The doors opened to Wonderland. Going to the movies was the most important thing that had then happened to me, apart, that is, from the incident on the haystack. Watching those wonderful films and stars of the late thirties and forties opened my eyes to what my life could be. I was never quite the same person after seeing Fred Astaire and Ginger Rogers dance; I think I wanted to be both of them. As for *Casablanca* and *Now Voyager*, well, from then on I knew exactly what I wanted to do with my life...be an actor.

One morning Mother asked me to go down to the bottom of the hill to buy a loaf of bread from the baker's. While I was in the shop 'Wailing Willie' went.

"Better cut back home quickly, Billy boy," said Mr Rodgers, the baker.

I did, mighty quickly; but while I was running up the hill I heard the noise of an aeroplane behind me. Turning round I saw a small German aircraft, a Messerschmitt, following me; it swooped down so low I could see the pilot in his leather helmet looking down at me. As I ran he fired. A great spatter of bullets exploded in the middle of the road by my side throwing up stones and earth. Terrified I dived into the ditch. When I got up I ran as fast as I'd ever done in my life. I didn't stop till I reached the safety of the cupboard under our stairs, clutching my loaf of bread, my heart beating as fast as the bobbin in Mother's sewing machine.

On the eve of her birthday, the night of the 22rd of March, when we were all sheltering in the Anderson at the bottom of the garden, there was an especially fearful explosion, the whole ground shook. A bomb had dropped exceedingly close by. Dust flew up from under the door, and the three ladies who were sheltering with us from next door stopped their knitting and fell to their knees in prayer. In the morning, after the All Clear sounded, we emerged into the dusty daylight to discover our house was not there. It had received a direct hit; there was nothing but rubble. We were homeless.

Chapter Eight

Evacuated

1941-42

I can see Mother on that bomb site now, dressed in her pink wool-
ly dressing gown and slippers, her hand clasped over her mouth
staring at what remained of our home. "Nothing!" she uttered.
"Not a stitch in the world but what we stand up in." Gathering
herself together, she muttered, "Right! First things first," and off
she went to tackle one of our neighbours. I was eleven years old
and had, by then, seen her crying many times, indeed copiously at
funerals. However, at this devastating catastrophe she shed not one
tear. She became practical, resourceful and sensible. Within ten
minutes she'd arranged where we would sleep that night and within half an hour had organised my future on a longer-term basis.
Mind you, never one to deny herself a drama, no sooner was she
off our neighbour's telephone than she was crawling over the ruins
wailing, "My furs! All my beautiful clothes gone! We'll have to
start all over." Rescuing whatever she could of her wardrobe and
picking up any pot or pan that could be useful, she added vehemently, "I'll murder that bloody Adolf Hitler, if I ever get my
hands on him."

Stan, by contrast, stood pole axed, blankly staring at the debris,
unable to say or do anything, which, I remember thinking, was
odd, for in his work he was used to investigating crashed aircraft
sites. I, with the insensibility of a child, was enthralled by the
shocking sight, curious to know what was going to happen to us
all.

Mother, like another of her screen heroines, Greer Garson in *Mrs Miniver*, had stoically risen above it all and arranged everything, perhaps not entirely to her satisfaction, for she was invited by Stan's widowed sister, Maud – whom I knew she loathed ("sanctimonious Maud" she used to call her), to stay in her grand manor house up in the Lake District. I was evacuated to Ayr in Scotland to stay with my Uncle Ralph and Auntie Pop-Goes-Your-Heart.

Relieved to be away from the bombs, it was refreshing to be in a house where I could leaf through books (in Mother's home there were rarely any, only *Picture Post* and her favourite fashion magazine, *Vogue*), where, over the dining table, there was talk of history and literature, for I was always captivated by stories. I thought Uncle Ralph a terrific chap. He was the nearest I had to a father figure, the only man around in my childhood I had any respect for; he was then stationed at 'H.M.S. Scotia' in Ayr, and it was from a beach nearby he taught me to swim. I attended Ayr Academy, which was a mixed school and I developed my second crush, this time on a girl, Sandra McLean. Sandra was a Nordic beauty who was in my class and sat at the desk directly in front of mine. She wore her yellow hair in one long plait which hung down in front of me and neatly fitted into my ink-pot. She was very angry with me when she discovered I was using it to paint Japanese hieroglyphics with, but I wooed her with gob-stoppers and she soon forgave me. We palled-up and went to the pictures together and even held hands. We watched *The Thief of Bagdad*, *Jungle Book*, and Alice Faye and Carmen Miranda musicals. We visited Alloway, the birthplace of Robert Burns, and Sandra taught me to recite his poems in a Scottish accent.

One sunny summer's afternoon walking home from school by way of the beach where I sometimes swam, the foaming white waves looked so inviting, I decided to go in for a dip. The trouble was I didn't have my swimming costume. I looked around ... not a soul... the beach was deserted. So I stripped off, leaving my clothes, including my underpants, on a rock with my school books, and dashed into the sea.

Ten minutes later when I came out, my clothes and books had vanished. The beach was still as deserted as it had been before, but now the sun had gone in behind the clouds. I ran the last quarter of a mile home stark naked, all along Achendoon Crescent, up Aroll Drive, with our neighbours in their front gardens looking up astonished as I whizzed past. Arriving at Uncle Ralph's bungalow I had no key, so, shivering and practically in tears, I rang the front door bell. Auntie Pop-Goes-Your-Heart opened the door. She took one look at the skinny eleven-year-old, clutching his winkle on her door step and roared with laughter. I was most put-out. I tried to explain what had happened as she wrapped me in a blanket, but she still carried on laughing even as she gave me a very welcome hot bath.

Mother sent me picture postcards of Lake Windermere and Coniston, saying what a "dear soul" Maud was to take them in, how "eternally grateful" she was, but "it's so very quiet up here in this huge house, it's driving me dotty. Give me London any day! We're planning to return to Croydon as soon as possible." Reading between the lines I guessed that it wasn't the quiet house that was driving her dotty, but 'sanctimonious Maud'.

Then one morning there was an envelope in her handwriting waiting for me on the doormat. In the letter Mother explained that she and Stan had been for a weekend walking trip with Maud into the Lake District, and Maud had "blown off and tragically fallen to her death."

What? I thought, hardly believing what I was reading. She's been at it again! Blown off, my foot! Pushed, more like. I could just see it. Maud standing alone on a cliff top looking out at the view. No Stan, no witnesses. Mother, full of hatred, creeping up behind her...one quick shove... and whoops! But when I spoke to Mother on the telephone later, she was tearful and seemed genuinely distraught. "It was such a gorgeous day," she related, "though I admit there was a bit of a breeze blowing as we got higher. We'd been walking for about an hour, in single file, you know. Stan in front, I was following and Maud was behind. All of a sudden there was a scream, I looked around and she was gone. Vanished into thin air, she had! Oh, it was just horrendous. Just disappeared off the face of the earth. We had to retrace our steps miles before we could get any help."

There were several articles in the newspapers about it. 'The Times' said, "Walker killed in mountain plunge", and our local 'Ayrshire Chronicle' headlined:

Woman dies after falling from ridge.

Maud Hunt, 39, from Carlisle, was out walking on Saturday at Striding Edge ridge, one of the most popular areas with walkers, when she was blown off the ridge and fell 813ft to her death. The Patterdale Mountain Rescue Team attended the scene and Mrs Hunt was flown in a Lawence Bell helicopter, but was pronounced dead. Inspector Ian Flower, who co-ordinated the rescue effort, warned walkers to be aware of the potential dangers of walking in the area."

It sounded plausible; maybe I was wrong; maybe the whole thing was in my imagination. But the thought of Stan's fat sister Maud being blown off anywhere, let alone a mountain ridge, just didn't convince me. I was tempted to confide my suspicions to Uncle Ralph, but with everyone being so sympathetic and kind – "Your poor dear mother and step-father, how awful for them," – with letters of condolence arriving almost every day, I lost confidence and kept silent. So there it was. If I was right, Mother had got away with murder again!

At least I was spared accompanying her to the funeral, at which, I was confidant she would have herself a ball and enjoy to the full her leading lady status. That position I always considered she subverted when she frequented other funerals, for she made such a song and dance she was inclined to upstage any genuinely grieving widow or female relative.

Soon afterwards she wrote saying they'd moved back to Croydon and that I was not to worry about her as she was now living and working with friends who ran "The Green Dragon," a public house in the High Street, and what is more, "we're really enjoying it. Meeting such a cross section of people across the bar and listening to their stories is fascinating. There are sing-songs every night with the soldiers on leave and I lead them with 'Roll out the barrel' and 'I've got a lovely bunch of coconuts'. We're really having great fun." I bet she was. I could just see her belting it out, kicking up her skirt and basking in the limelight.

After Christmas she wrote again telling me she'd enrolled me as a boarder for the Spring Term at Brighton College, a minor public school in Sussex, but I had to first undergo an interview with the Headmaster. So down south I came in the train, leaving, as I look back on it now, one of the happiest periods of my childhood.

She met me at Euston Railway Station with a tall man she introduced as 'Mr Dancy'. Mr William Dancy wore a camel-haired coat, had tight greasy curls at the back of his neck and owned a big Wolseley car. I sat on the expensive-smelling leather upholstery at the back while he drove us to Fuller's Tea Rooms in Croydon. During the course of conversation it became apparent that he was a greengrocer or 'market gardener', as he called himself, and lived on the Sussex Downs.

"This is the man you were named after," Mother said coyly as we were having tea. I didn't quite know how to react to that. What on earth was she trying to tell me? That this man was my biological father? She simpered and flirted with him outrageously, then, squeezing my ear lobe and smoothing my unruly hair – which was something she always did and always irritated me – asked him, "And what do think of my gorgeous big son?"

I don't think Mr Dancy knew quite how to react to that either, for he stared at me poker-faced. "Like football, do you?"

"Not much," I answered.

He frowned and asked. "What do you like, then?"

"Films, mostly. Musicals, dancing... Rita Hayworth, Betty Grable."

At the mention of Miss Grable his handsome fleshy face creased into a grin. "Ah, now you're talking. The boy's obviously got taste."

"You haven't changed!" Mother quipped, and to me added, "Just walked into the bar the other night, he did. Hadn't seen each other for nearly fourteen years, had we? Right out of the blue and there he was... large as life and twice as handsome!"

Mr Dancy winked at me. "Well, couldn't forget those legs, could I?"

Whether it was because I'd not seen Mother for a year or because I was that bit older, I was able to detect in her a nervousness I'd never noticed before. She touched her face and hair rather too often, she seemed to be a mess of superficiality – which was something I'd gradually become aware of – yet now there was something else. She looked as wonderful as ever in some navy and white polka-dotted dress, but her exaggerated emotions and obvious anxiety to please this fellow who I took to be no more than a spiv, betrayed a sort of desperation. I noticed they gave each other a very gooey kiss when they parted and I wondered what 'Pop' Stan would have to say about it if he knew.

Chapter Nine

Clytemnestra

1942-1950

Fearfully, I gazed awestruck, at the nineteenth century entrance arch to Brighton College. I was twelve years old and it seemed to me as I looked at the forbidding flint-stone building beyond, that it was the Tower of London and I would be walking through Traitor's Gate. Mother took my hand and together we walked under the archway. We were shown the school chapel, the swimming pool and sports field. Then I had my interview with the headmaster, Mr Stafford-Clarke in his study. With his polished hair, haughty manner and impeccable stiff white collar, he was the most intimidating and grandest gentleman I'd ever met. After our talk I sat for a written test with three other boys.

A week later we were informed I had been accepted as a boarder.

Mother and Stan moved to Warlingham in Surrey where they took over a pub that stood on the village green, 'The Leather Bottle'.

"Barlett's mother is a barmaid!" jeered one of my snobbish new classmates. This was my first encounter with class distinction and I was at a loss. I clenched my middle-class fist and punched the boy on the nose. It bled magnificently, but it didn't make me feel any better.

By this time I'd become a good swimmer and even a junior champion diver. When Mother appeared on Speech Day to witness my prowess in the pool, the snobs changed their tune. "Wow!

Barlett's mother's a corker, did you see her?" and "Barlett's ma looks like a film star." Extraordinarily, as I look back on it now, I was as proud of these comments about Mother, as I was of my diving medals.

I sang in the school choir and during one Sunday morning service was surprised to notice William Dancy sitting in the congregation. Afterwards we met in the quad.

"How are you, young fellow m'lad?" he said clapping me on the back. "Y'mother suggested I come and take you out for the day. Come and join my family for lunch. Meet my boys."

He drove me to his farmhouse on the Downs and, after Mrs Dancy had given us lunch, we went for a walk with his dogs around his estate. I was uncomfortable and didn't know what to say to him. Why was I here? What did he want with me? We played cricket with his young sons on the lawn and, before taking me back to school, we had a strawberry cream tea. The visit could not have gone off very well for I was never invited again.

It was not until I was in my twenties and living in London that I saw him again. I was just about to cross a zebra crossing by South Kensington tube station when a Rolls Royce stopped allowing me to pass. I glanced up at the driver and it was Mr Dancy, beside him sat my mother. Our eyes met but she completely blanked me. Married to her third husband, old Joe Walsh at the time, I immediately realised it was infidelity with a stony face.

Many years later she told me William Dancy had died and she asked me to accompany her to his funeral. "Only if you promise to be tactful," I said, "and not parade your grief."

"Under the circumstances I'm hardly likely to do that," she replied crossly.

So we went. There I met his widow, Mrs Dancy, again, and their two grown-up sons. William Dancy had been a tall man; but, as very soon became apparent, the grave diggers had not dug a long enough grave, so when the coffin was lowered, it didn't fit. The burial service had to be conducted with Mr Dancy propped up in his coffin at an angle. By the graveside Mother behaved herself admirably but, as soon as we got into the car, she collapsed with helpless laugher. "He was erect as ever," she hooted, "until the very end, bless him!"

Auntie Linda, of 'Philinda' fame, still lived in Brighton; she was a cosy soul who had married a sailor, or so she told me, though he was never at home when I visited her in her untidy flat on my Sundays off from school. Her father, Mr Thompson, a kindly old gentleman I seemed to have known most of my life, also lived with her. Linda used to cook me Sunday lunch then sign my 'Leave Out Pass', which allowed me to go into the town alone for my weekly treat, a visit to the pictures. One Sunday while she was doing the washing up in the kitchen, Mr Thompson, sitting on the sofa in the living room, calmly opened my fly buttons, took out my john thomas and proceeded to give me a blow job; that was the afternoon I saw *Gilda*, I recall. I went to the pictures every Sunday afternoon but never allowed Mr Thompson to do that again. I endured the same thing from my diction teacher, too, but he was an old actor called Henry Baynton who sandwiched his fellatio sessions with thrilling stories of Shakespeare's plays, so I didn't mind it that much.

Then those atomic bombs went off in Hiroshima and Nagasaki and the war finally finished. There were celebrations but we still had rationing. The wounds of war slowly began to heal and the world gradually, very gradually, started to change. At the time, living in the sheltered walls of an English public school, I barely noticed, for an explosion of a rather different sort had gone off in my head jolting me from my vow to forget all I'd heard from under the bed. It happened was while I was studying Homer's *Odyssey*. Of the many marvellous stories therein, the one that struck home for me was that of the hero Agamemnon and how, when he returned home from the Trojan War, he was slain by his wife Clytemnestra. Her son, Orestes, punished her with death.

I had just as much cause as Orestes, I thought, so how could I best accomplish it? And, more importantly, how could I get away with it? Preposterous maybe, but at the time I was in deadly earnest. Murderous thoughts curdled around my imaginative brain. Plots like pouring poison into Mother's ear while she was asleep, as Claudius does in *Hamlet*. I knew she loved picnics; maybe I could persuade her to have one on top of Beachy Head and push her off? Better still, push her in front of an underground train. Stab her? But then, there was my floppy-dagger-dream problem. Strangle her? Yes, that'd be best... looking into her face and telling her why, and what a wicked woman she was. I dismissed the notion of a poisoned letter as being too complicated, so I decided the school holidays would be the best time. These macabre reveries occurred rather inappropriately while I was rehearsing the title role of Bernard Shaw's *St Joan*. Being a member of the school Play Reading Society and the winner of a verse-speaking contest, I'd managed to persuade my Housemaster, who directed our end of term plays, into casting me in his productions. So I also played Mrs Jones in Galsworthy's *The Silver Box*, the miser in Moliere's *The Miser*, Calpurnia in *Julius Caesar*, Miranda the mermaid, and an American chorus girl, Rene La Lune in Alec Copel's *I Killed the Count*. As you see, an eclectic selection not, unfortunately, followed through in my professional career. One of my school reports read, 'Bartlett would do better if he were more interested in History than histrionics.'

I wrote to Mother telling her of my plan of going on the stage. I could just see the scene at home when my letter arrived:

"Billy writes that he wants to be an actor!" said Mother at the breakfast table.

"Good God!" exclaimed Stan, from behind his 'Daily Mail'. "He'll be sitting down to wee-wee next!"

"Must you be so coarse?" she answered, barely glancing up from my letter. "He says he's started elocution lessons!"

"How much is that going to cost us?"

"He says there's a famous old actor who comes in once a week and gives private classes, a 'Henry Baynton'."

"Never heard of him!" said Stan, turning his paper to the racing section. "Well, I suppose it's an improvement on him prancing around wanting to be a dancer."

"Why are you so against it? I wanted to go on the stage myself, you know I did. I expect he gets it from me. I wanted to be a singer....and you do have to be trained for that sort of life. Anyway, we can afford it now, what with the fortune dear Maud left us."

"Left me, dear; left to me!"

"Well, her inheritance. Bless her!"

"That's not how you used to refer to her."

"Well, the poor dear's dead now, isn't she? I never speak ill of the dead, I only speak good. Maud Hunt is dead. Good!"

When I returned home for the school holidays she presented me with a leather-bound copy of the *Complete Works of William Shakespeare* and an application form for an audition to the Royal Academy of Dramatic Art. She actually came with me to the audition, not that I wanted her to; she was the one who insisted on coming. With the fearlessness of youth and buoyed up by my successes in school plays (well, I was only sixteen), I breezed through the experience with aplomb. I do recall, however, seeing my fellow auditionees pacing nervously and one girl actually being sick. Happily I passed and was accepted into the Academy. Mother was as ecstatic with excitement as I was, so my plans to kill her rather ebbed away. I was still filled with anger against her but my own life had suddenly become more interesting.

I spent the next two years in an orgy of theatricals. Learning speeches, learning plays, acting in them, having fencing lessons, movement and diction classes, (this was before 'kitchen-sink' dramas and regional accents became the fashion), learning about stage technique, make-up, and the most riveting extracurricular activity ever, sex.

Grown-ups, good-looking guys out of the Forces and gorgeous girls – some of whom in those days used RADA as a finishing school – were my fellow students, and I was a walking hormonal erection, up for shagging everything in sight. Fortunately many seemed to be of a similar frame of mind and I'm happy to report reciprocated my feelings. No one then seemed to be bothered about commitment or even health care and I enjoyed myself enormously. I seemed to have had no hang-up whatever about sex; queer, straight, it never bothered me – that all came later – like an excited puppy I romped and coupled with whoever was interested. As the Americans say, I was young, dumb and full of cum. No, my only hang-up was about Mother.

Attempting to conform or maybe searching for my identity, I dressed in the de-rigueur outfit of drama students of the day, a yellow polo-neck sweater, bottle-green corduroys and open-toed sandals. Waving me off one morning to catch the commuter train to Victoria, Mother eyed me curiously and observed, "You must be different, mustn't you?" which I thought was rich coming from her.

She never came to any of my performances, which, at the time, disappointed me. Then slowly it dawned on me... she was jealous.

During my first vacation from the R.A.D.A. I joined an amateur dramatic group in Streatham; I played 'Dickey Winslow', *The Winslow Boy*'s elder brother and helped to paint the scenery with another boy, Charlie, who became my best friend. He was slightly older than me and was training to be an architect. We borrowed an eighteen-foot-long yacht from a friend and sailed it up the Thames from Chertsey, sleeping in a tent. Apart from the policeman at East Croydon Police station, he was the only person to whom I ever admitted what I'd heard from under the bed. "I think my Ma suffocated my Dad with a pillow," I confessed to him one night in our tent.

"My Dad killed my Mum, too," he answered blithely. "Killed himself, too, in a car crash." As that seemed far more dramatic than my story, I never mentioned it again.

A B.B.C. director came to see my last show at the Academy and afterwards offered me a television series about juvenile delinquents, but at eighteen I was obliged to do my National Service.

Having spent two years leaning how essential individuality is to an actor – 'Anyone can play Hamlet, it's your personality that makes it special', – I didn't intend ditching it all in favour of learning how to become an automaton and 'kill to order', which is how my friend Charlie, who was now stationed at Cattarick army barracks, had written describing his training. So, putting my new-found acting studies to work, I studied the behaviour of schizophrenics and attended my medical with a large wooden crucifix round my neck. This I gripped fanatically while standing stark bollock naked, pleading, "You must let me in. I have to save those poor boys."

Despite the fact I was bursting with good health, my plan worked. I was rejected on 'Medical grounds' so the letter said, and I was able to take up my B.B.C. contract.

All Mother said after seeing me on television as a juvenile delinquent was, "What a pity you didn't play a nice part, in a suit."

She was good at the dysphoric put-down. I learnt to play the piano, and as I practised Beethoven's Moonlight Sonata she reflected wistfully, "What I wouldn't give if you could play the piano like Charlie Kunz."

I answered an advertisement in *The Stage*: 'A.S.M. Juvenile. Summer Season, Pier Theatre, Bognor Regis,' and landed my first theatre job. Lesley Hammond, our stout middle-aged actor-manager played all the leading parts. I painted the scenery, collected the props and prompted, all for £4.10 shillings a week, but I was the happiest teenager in the world. A 12" x 10" photograph of my eighteen-year-old face moodily scowling at the world in a crew-necked sweater with my hair Brylcreamed like a young Tony Curtis was put on show in the front of the theatre. I can honestly report that though I'd never considered myself handsome, when I first saw this picture I realised that, decently lit, from the right angle, with my hair combed, I could look quite dashing, which seemed to be confirmed by the groups of girls that started waiting outside the stage door in the evenings for my autograph. This had an extraordinarily good effect on me, Confidence, being one of the main qualities required of an actor. The other absolute necessities, in my opinion, are Timing – which I knew I had; Imagination – of which I possibly had too much; Charisma – well, he said, modestly, that's for others to say; and Health – mercifully that has seldom been a problem. This was all pre-*Look Back in Anger* days and I bounced through many a wobbly French window in white flannels, beaming "Anyone for tennis?"

I lived in a caravan and, while playing 'Laertes' to the overweight Mr Hammond's 'Hamlet', became deeply enamoured of the virgin playing 'Ophelia', a fact I unwisely confided to Mother – not the virgin part – in a tea shop on the front after a matinee. All she said about my performance was: "Laertes! If I'd known that's all you were playing I'd never have come. I thought you were playing Hamlet!"

Ophelia joined us for tea. Mother complimented her on her performance, she complimented Mother on her jewels and handbag.

Mother probed, trying to place her status. The virgin shied and promptly departed, "So the two of you can have a moment."

Mother looked at me with a sinister expression. "Are you serious about that girl?"

"Very," I answered.

"Huh!" she snorted. "So that's why I've not heard from you for months." Then, eyeing me suspiciously, "Are you living with her?"

"Of course not!"

"Don't look so shocked, people do, you know. You never know anyone till you live with them. I wish to God I had. I'd have soon found out about your father."

At the mention of Father I bit my tongue, for I had devised a cunning plan.

"Well," she persisted, "are you thinking of marrying this girl?"

"Maybe," I replied.

"Don't be ridiculous, you're far too young, anyway she reeks of B.O."

I stared, astonished.

"Oh, she had a nice handbag, I'll give her that, but, oh dear me, no. Hands like hams, fingers like sausages; you couldn't possibly marry her!"

Looking at the size of Ophelia's fingers that evening, I had to agree.

The devilish plan I had conceived was born during our *Hamlet* rehearsals, listening to his speech:

I have heard that guilty creatures sitting at a play
Have by the very cunning of the scene
Been struck so to the soul that presently
They have proclaimed their malefactions;
For murder, though it have no tongue, will speak
With most miraculous organ.

Why not, I thought, do the same thing before Mother? Play something like the murder of my father before her? Write a play about Clytemnestra killing her husband Agamemnon – I'd play that part – then watch her being, as Hamlet says: *struck to the soul*. Except that, if I was playing the dead king with my eyes shut, I couldn't very well do that... no, no, I'd have to play another part and be free to scrutinise her behaviour during the scene. If it worked out, Mother would reveal her part in his death and I'd have my revenge. Yes, I'll do it. 'The play's the bomb wherein I'll catch the conscience of my mom'.

On Christmas Day at home it had become a tradition that I produce a pantomime or show of some kind. I decided that that would be the ideal time. Mother came from a family of seven; she had three brothers and three sisters, so there was usually one of them staying with us at the time with their respective husband or wife and offspring; my cousins, whom I dragooned into helping with the show. I plotted that next Christmas, which was only a few months away, we would perform the murder of King Agamemnon by his wife Clytemnestra; I would play their son Orestes and kill her in revenge. So I started to write.

The problem was it was a Greek tragedy and hardly suitable fair to follow the King's speech on Christmas Day. Also Clytemnestra had stabbed her husband; I needed to have her suffocate him if Mother's conscience was to be successfully pricked. My adulation of Lana Turner and Barbara Stanwyck came to my aid. The story became a mixture of *Double Indemnity* and *The Postman Always Rings Twice* and, since I chose Tchaikovsky's "Romeo and Juliet Fantasy Overture" with its terrific climax as the background music, a fantasy in mime is exactly what it became.

I don't think the audience realised quite what had hit them. There were six of them sitting in the lounge, all replete from hearty portions of Christmas fare. There was Mother, 'Pop' Stan, my

Auntie Evelyn and Uncle Len, the barmaid, and some man friend of Mother's who always seemed to be around. I dimmed the lights allowing only the adjusted table lamps to shine on the scene. Ina, my tall fifteen-year old cousin, played Clytemnestra wearing a long nightie, a great deal of lipstick and a wobbly pair of high-heels. My seventeen-year-old cousin, Trevor, played King Agamemnon – supposedly my father – with a cardboard crown and a false moustache, both of which kept slipping off. I was so cross at their non-professional antics I almost forgot to watch Mother, who, totally bewildered by our antics, spent most of the time chatting to her sister, Evelyn. When it came to the pillow-suffocating scene, Ina crept forward in the way I had instructed her, and pressed the cushion over Trevor's sleeping head. I was standing at the side, my eyes, like a hawk's, riveted to Mother's face. At last she was frozen in attention. Any moment, I knew she would react and give herself away by fainting or doing something dramatic. Then Trevor ruined it all by choking, "I can't breathe!" and everyone laughed.

Mother actually stood up like Claudius does in the play scene in *Hamlet*, but didn't shout, "Give me some light: away!" Mundanely she called out, "Are you alright, Trevor? Have a glass of water, dear."

The rest of the show was rather a let-down. In the next scene I entered as Orestes and throttled Ina, but the Tchaikovsky record had run out by then so I had to do it in silence which wasn't nearly so effective.

Tepid applause followed my performance and Mother muttered, "Well, I've no idea what that was all about," and started passing round mince pies.

So that was the end of that. I was still as far away as ever from solving my Mother problem, but on the other hand, Life and 'Showbiz' had a great deal more to offer a red-blooded young man than a murderous Mum and rep on the end of the pier at Bognor Regis.

Chapter Ten

Holiday Romance

1951

I spent my twenty-first birthday in Venice. By then I'd completed another repertory season in Carlisle, where I'd played leading parts, also a play and two revues in what these days we'd call the London fringe.

Venice was a formative and thrilling time.

I was accompanying the distinguished and cultured director of my last play and the revues, Norman Marshall. Norman was a delightful fellow, a witty, sophisticated and civilized man of the world; he had an easy warmth and appeared to know just about everyone who was anyone. He took me to museums, endless churches and galleries, opening my eyes and elevating my perceptions of painting and architecture. He taught me about wines, how to tell a Bordeaux claret from a Burgundy, how to conduct myself in grand houses, and, most important of all, he taught me good taste in the theatre. He called me his protégé and took pride in polishing me up. In those days breeding and class, or assuming it, were essential if you had any sort of ambition to work in the West End theatre, and that, I had aplenty. He introduced me to Sybil Thorndike – Shaw's original *St Joan*; to Gertrude Lawrence and Noel Coward – to whom I shyly said, "I thought *Brief Encounter* was absolutely super, sir," to which he replied, "I'm so glad when someone young likes my work. I thought you all thought I was a pink sausage left over from the twenties"; and to Vivien Leigh, whom I artlessly asked, "What's it like being famous?" She answered, "Augustus John calls you up and asks if he can paint you." I met writers, artists and a host of socialite grandees, and one evening we were asked to dinner by Peggy Guggenheim.

Norman explained, "Peggy is the doyenne art connoisseur and socialite of New York, Paris and Venice. Her gondola will call for us at seven thirty and take us to her Palazzo Venier dei Leoni on the Grand Canal. On her walls you're going to see some of the best modern paintings in the world."

It wasn't until her gondola appeared at our hotel quay – a glossy black and gold affair with awnings dripping with tassels and luxury, and even more eye catching, her gondolier, a tall, stunningly handsome man with jet-black hair and olive skin, dressed in white with a turquoise sash around his waist – that I realised we were in for an evening of exceptional interest.

Miss Guggenheim turned out to be a white-haired matronly lady who combined sophistication with coziness. She greeted us with Pekinese dogs in her wake; taking my arm she immediately put me at my ease. Her sitting room was fifties bohemian, white leather couches, black and white rugs. Dinner was an informally grand affair, eight other guests including a loquacious Truman Capote – before he wrote *Breakfast at Tiffany's*. There was crystal glass and rivers of champagne and, as Norman had apprised me, Picassos, Miros, Braques, Chagalls, Magrittes and Dalis hanging on her walls. The talk was of Art and travel, celebrities and adultery; I was struck dumb, numb on a pink cloud of culture, elegance, and sophistication.

A week later I developed an ear ache; some bug, it appeared, had infected my ear while I'd been swimming in the Lido. Norman called in a doctor who gave me an injection and said "This boy is unfit to fly." We were due to return home the following morning, Norman had to start work on a new production, so what to do with me?

"I'll call Peggy," he said.

He came back from the phone grinning. "She's leaving for New York this afternoon, but said if you're the sweet English boy I brought to dinner, you're very welcome to stay at the Palazzo. Giovanni, her gondolier, will call for you tomorrow morning."

At ten o'clock the following morning, the gorgeous Giovanni, a cross between a young Elvis Presley and Warren Beatty came to my bed-side. I was only wearing pyjama bottoms and still felt somewhat groggy, my left ear and the side of my face were absolutely numb. He picked me up in his arms and carried me down the stairs into his golden gondola. Norman followed with the cases. Arriving at the Palazzo, Giovanni carried me up the steps and inside, setting me down on a chaise-longue by a window. Norman and I said our farewells and he caught the water bus to the airport from the steps of the Palazzo. I clearly remember noticing the water lapping his shoes and the turn-ups of his trousers as he waved me goodbye.

I lay back gazing at my surroundings. I was in an airy ornate room overlooking the glittering Grand Canal, opposite was the Prefecture and the white domed Salute. Gondolas were bobbing; there was the noise of vaporettos and the heavenly sight of the Venice skyline. Suddenly, without a sound, Giovanni appeared at my side.

"Is there anything I can do for you, Signor?"

"Perfavor la toilette?" I struggled.

He put his arm under mine and escorted me through a concealed door. We entered what at first seemed a black ice palace. It was in fact an Italian marble bathroom, but I barely noticed the gold taps or black marble sink or clocked that it was a bathroom at all. The entire room, including the ceiling, was covered in a sort of translucent tile, each of a different mix of squashed blue and green, mirrored black and gold. I peered curiously at the wall trying to distinguish how the effect was achieved and saw, reflected back, Giovanni at my side. He still had his arm under mine, but he was now nibbling my ear...only I couldn't feel him.

I turned and looked into his intense black eyes.

He kissed me tenderly with his full young maroon lips.

My knees went weak...I literally zonked out.

The rest of my stay in Venice seems like a half-remembered dream. Giovanni waited on me while I recovered – pretty swiftly, I might add – on the chaise-longue. We listened to the radio, and, when I was better, danced to Renato Carosone records, cha-cha-cha-ing before Picasso's 'La Beignole'. We tried to explain and talk about ourselves in our fractured English and Italian. He told me he liked woman to sleep and have sex with, but men to love. However he was very happy to sleep and have sex with me in the double bed Miss Guggenheim had so very generously provided.

I was quite hypnotised by his masculine beauty, his lean muscular body, the symmetry of his features, his tilted nose, the tips of his lips, his dark lashed smoky eyes. His hair, thick and black, was combed into a quiff with a curl falling at the centre of his forehead. I suppose there must have been other staff around, for delicious food appeared, but I have no recollection of anyone other than him and how for a week I loved him.

As we said our goodbyes at the airport, me, the returning tourist in my navy Aquascutum suit trying to ignore the lump in my throat, Giovanni's moist eyes searched mine for some sort of reassurance. We promised letters and further visits, but it was not until I was in my seat and airborne that I suspected our promises might be broken and I would never see him again.

Back in London I wrote a bread-and-butter letter to Miss Guggenheim thanking her for her hospitality and commending Giovanni's nursing.

But I could not forget him. Every time I saw a Canaletto painting, a Guardi, a Murillo, a Ghislandi, an Alexandro or Pietro Longi, a Tiepolo, or even saw a photograph of Venice, I remembered Giovanni and that week of happiness he gave me.

Our affair – I do so loathe that word, it savours of decadence and back-stairs shenanigans, whereas, at the time my feelings were of something fine and noble – had the effect of making me feel very differently about myself. I soon realised it had been a purely physical attraction and the two of us could hardly have made a life together, but I also knew that, for the first time in my life, something deep within me had been touched, something very close to love. It seemed to me then to be a clear indication of my true nature and was likely to become my way of life, which, in the dark ages of 1951 – two years before Sir John Gielgud, one of the most distinguished actors in the world would be arrested for 'cottaging' – was a very big problem indeed.

As if having a murderess for a Mother wasn't problem enough.

Chapter Eleven

Confession

1976/1956-57

My car wheels splashed into a glistening puddle under the street lamp as I rounded the corner into Parson's Green, my road just off the King's Road, Fulham. Home was a semi-detached Victorian house that Annie and I had bought when we were first married, it had tall ceilings, three bedrooms and a really splendid south-facing back garden. A warm welcoming light filtered through the stained glass front door. I turned the key. Delicious cooking smells assailed my nostrils.

Annie, wearing an apron, was stirring something in the kitchen.

"Darling!" she said, air kissing my cheek, "Good day?" Without waiting for an answer she launched into a catalogue of her day's events. "The Garden Centre people delivered the wood for the decking. It's in the garden with some wondrous plants. The carpenter is due tomorrow morning, so if you're still going to see your mother, you'd better leave him that drawing we made. The other news is really special. I've been offered a fabulous part in a new telly serial."

"Annie!" I said. "That's terrific. What is it?"

"An adaptation of a novel... on location... all on film... starts next month, it'll be a nightmare to organize the children, we'll have to get a nanny in, but I'm thrilled. This nosh will take another ten minutes. Pop up and say good night to them, James wants to tell you something."

Both my children were sitting up in their beds reading, though I suspected Rebecca had heard me coming and had just scampered in. James, my nine-year-old son, freshly-bathed with his hair washed, looked just like an angel-boy in soap commercial. "Dadda!" he said. "I made two goals and Mr Gilligan marked me down in his book and said I had the best score of all the juniors."

"That comes as no surprise to me, bubba," I said sitting on his bed. "Congratulations."

Turning to Rebecca, who, at twelve years old was well on her way to becoming a tousled-haired tomboy, I asked, "How did your teacher like the green painting of the trees and the car you took to school?"

Grinning, thrilled that I'd remembered, she replied, "She pinned it up in the classroom and said if I could do another one like it, I might grow up to be a proper artist."

"I told you it was good one. She's right. If you want to be, you will be."

"How long are you going to be at Grandma's?" said James.

"Not long. Only for a day or two."

"Can we go and see the dinosaur afterwards?"

"I promise. Snuggle down, now."

I tucked them both in, kissed them goodnight, and went to the bathroom for a shower. During supper Annie filled me in on the details of her new job. I dozed while watching the results of the American Presidential election on television, Jimmy Carter had just beat Gerald Ford to the White House, and afterwards I stumbled into bed. Freed from having to remember lines – I always learned them last thing at night – I fell into that blissful black velvet pit of sleep unimpeded. Thus my subconscious, for a better understanding of the present, was at liberty to continue combing through the past.

In my twenties I made a conscious decision to keep Mother at arm's length. I was so busy working and trying to make a career for myself it wasn't too difficult. I made some films, playing small parts in comedies at Pinewood studios. I did some television: *Z Cars* and *Dixon of Dock Green*, for two years I was on the road touring the provinces in torrid plays, sometimes playing twice nightly. I visited her only between jobs and then only for the odd weekend.

With Maud's inheritance Stan bought himself a pub of his own. "The Olive Branch" was, and still is, a warm and cosy public house that was founded in the 1500's; it stands in the corner of the Old Butter Market opposite the entrance to the great Canterbury Cathedral. One Saturday afternoon I arrived there to find the two of them were not on speaking terms.

"What on earth's happened?" I asked Mother on Sunday afternoon while Stan was out playing billiards. Enthroned on her favourite Queen Anne chair in the first floor living room, her four Pekinese dogs snuffling at her feet, she was manicuring her nails. At her side was a table covered with all the attendant paraphernalia, bottles of nail polish in shades from 'Pale Rose' to 'Jungle Red'. "Well," she said, gearing herself up to tell the tale. "The other day I was in the town shopping..." dipping her manicure brush into a pot, she held her breath, concentrating on covering her nail with Chinese Red with the utmost care... completed, she breathed again. "Fenwick's, you know the department store in St George's Lane. I was actually looking for a new bra and hoping to find one in the lingerie department." Admiring her glistening thumb nail, she daintily turned it to me. "Do you like the colour?"

"Lovely, Mother."

"Anyway," she continued, meticulously proceeding to another talon. "The lady behind the counter, who I happen to know slightly, came up wreathed in smiles and asked, 'Did you like the negligee your husband gave you for your birthday last week?'" Mother's imitation of the cloying vendeuse was biting. "Well, as my birthday is in March, as you know, and it's now October, bells rang! 'Yes,' I lied, hoping to encourage the wretched woman to disclose a little more, 'it was delightful.' Playing for time I toyed with some flimsy piece of rayon rubbish they had lying on the counter.

'I'm so glad,' said the woman, 'because he didn't know what size you were or anything. Typical man! So I recommended one of my favourites.'

'Thank you so much,' I answered, sweetly, 'a perfect choice.'

"Well, as you can imagine, my suspicions were well and truly aroused. Directly I got home I went straight to the spare room opposite the kitchen, that's where Valerie, our part-time barmaid sleeps at weekends. Sure enough, under her pillow, there it was. A disgusting black lace nightie! Well, it all clicked into place. I'd been wondering why he took so bloody long when he went down to the kitchen to make me a cup of tea in the morning. He was popping in to her bedroom opposite for a not-very-quick kiss and cuddle, the bugger. So I promptly had it out with him. 'What's all this?' I asked, brandishing the filthy thing in front of his eyes. He was lost for words. Lost for words he was, didn't know where to put himself. Guilty conscience, you see. I went upstairs to our bedroom, took his pyjamas from under his pillow and flung them down the stairs. 'You don't come back into my bedroom till you come back on your knees,' I said to him. 'On your knees, crawling through that door!'"

I wasn't around to see if 'Pop' did actually crawl through the door on his knees, or to witness Mother's triumphant expression as he did so, but he must have done it, for when I returned a month later, he was back sleeping in the marital bed. Valerie, the raven-haired barmaid was sacked, and her name was forbidden to be mentioned ever again.

Since my Venice escapade it was clear to me which side of the sexual fence I'd fallen, but I was far from happy about it. I had minor sexual exploits, but nothing to rival my relationship with Giovanni, not, that is, until after that very weekend with Mother.

I had signed on for a tour of a new production and at the first reading fell head-long in lust with a fellow actor in the company. I say 'lust' with hindsight, for at the time I was convinced it was the real thing. To make matters worse he was married and we shared a dressing room. Every night as we prepared for the show he sat next to me practically naked. He was a beautiful man, masculine, funny, a terrific actor and I adored him. He became the centre of all my thought. However there was no earthly way he was going to reciprocate my feelings, in the first place he didn't have a clue how I felt. The best acting I ever did was with him in the dressing room. I became so butch, pretending to be an ardent football fan, learning the names of all the Arsenal players, because that was his favourite team. I talked about girls and how I fancied them. My emotions were in turmoil with the total agony of loving someone I knew would never love me back. His wife visited us several times. She was lovely, as were their two children, and the whole awkward business of being a homosexual really hit me. Believing that I was in an impossible situation, and thinking it unlikely I would ever be able to find true love and happiness, I became suicidal and seriously considered blowing my brains out, or, as I didn't possess a gun, turning on the gas. Deeply unhappy I went home to Mother.

Lying on the sofa on Sunday in her over-heated living room after lunch, I tried to concentrate on reading a book. She was enthroned as usual on her Queen Anne chair absorbed in her ritual of manicuring her nails. I found myself yearning to confide in her. After all, she, very probably, had something to do with the way I was. I'd read enough books on the subject of homosexuality to know the theory that dominating mothers without dads produced effeminate boys. So successful had I become at appearing to be the very opposite – I was now muscular, aggressive and athletic – that playing the part of toughies and delinquent teenagers was now becoming my professional bread and butter.

Stan was out as usual playing billiards, there was a concert playing on the radio, her Pekinese dogs were sleeping peacefully at her feet and there was a rare relaxed feeling between us.

"How's that pretty girlfriend of yours?" she asked. "The one with the sausage fingers?"

"I've no idea, Mother. I haven't seen her for yonks."

"What a pity. She was lovely, a good actress, too. I thought at one time you might have married her."

Here was my cue. Yes, go for it. "Don't worry, Mother. I'll never marry." I took a deep breath. "I'm homosexual."

She froze. Holding her nail polish brush in mid-air she glared at me with a frenzied expression. Slowly, deliberately, she returned it to the pot, screwing it carefully back on. She shut her eyes and murmured, "Oh, my God! What have I done?" There was a pause, and then lifting her head up she howled like a wolf. "NOOOOOOOOOOOOOOOOOOO!"

Awoken by the sudden yowl, the dormant Pekes sprang to life; all four of them started yapping, snapping and barking. The concert on the radio was Tchaikovsky's '1812 Overture', at this point the fireworks and cannons crashed and roared. Simultaneously the bells from Canterbury Cathedral abruptly clanged to life with a deafening peel. The cacophony of noise was ear-splitting. The heavens were crashing in on me.

"What have I done to deserve this?" she demanded of the Almighty. "Now I'll never have grandchildren. That's all I've been living for all these years. The only thing I've ever wanted. Now you tell me this ghastly thing. That a son of mine...a son of mine. For God's sake stop that barking, Ming!" With a well-aimed kick her shoe landed on Ming Lou's rear. The yelping whelp vanished under the table. "What am I to do?" she continued. "Oh, Lord, I'll never get over this."

I tried to stay calm. "Just think, Mother, you'll never lose me to another woman. You'll have me all my life. No woman will ever come between us."

"That's all very well for you but what about my grandchildren? I've yearned for the day I had grandchildren, and now, never, never! That's all I've ever asked from life. I could never have any more babies after you were born. You ripped the womb right out of me, you bugger. Right out of me. Nearly killed me, you did. Oh, you're so wicked to do this to me, so selfish." Gathering up the grizzling Peke she cooed, "Sorry my baby, did Mummy hurt you, then? Never mind, come to Mummy then."

There was not a word said about how I might be feeling, it was really quite funny in a sickening sort of way.

"I don't know how I'm ever going to get over this," she announced again cuddling Ming, then suddenly as the thought struck, "For God's sake don't tell Stan. It would kill him... Just kill him!" She groaned, sobbed, and gasped some more.

"Mother, please." I leant over to placate and embrace her.

"Don't touch me," she cried, freezing. "Take your hands off me. You give me the shivers." Nuzzling Ming to her cheek she enquired of it, "What a dreadful boy, he is, isn't he, my darling? A dreadful boy." Turning to me she added vehemently, "As far as I'm concerned, it would have been better if you'd never been born."

Oh dear! I had raised a high wall between us. I left the room and went for a walk. The subject, like Valerie, the raven-haired barmaid, was never referred to again.

Chapter Twelve

A Hat Trick

1958

Six months later, it was a Monday afternoon I remember, I was at the Theatre Royal, Newcastle- upon-Tyne, touring in some god-forsaken drama giving another of my cosh boy performances – I was in danger of becoming type-cast – but in this play, at least, mine was the star role. Just as I was making myself at home for the week, placing my make-up things neatly on a towel before the mirror in my number one dressing-room, the phone rang.

"Mrs Mackey for you, sir," said the stage-door keeper.

My agent, Mrs Mackey from the Al Parker agency in Mount Street, Park Lane, never telephoned unless she had a job or an interview for me to attend, so I waited for her to be put through with a certain degree of excitement.

"Billy!" Mrs Mackey's crisp voice called down the line. "Are you there?"

"Hello, how are you?"

"Darling, I've had a call from your mother. She didn't know which city you were playing this week. Apparently your step-father has just died." Mrs Mackey didn't waste words on non-professional matters. "She wants you to call her."

"Oh, yes, of course. Er... How are things? I mean work-wise, anything happening?"

"I'll let you know if anything pops up. Anyway, you're busy. Enjoying the tour?"

"Loving it."

"Good. Condolences, my darling boy. You take care, Poppet."

And she was gone.

I asked the stage-door keeper to dial me Mother's number. As I waited, I tried not to let my mind go sour and think the worse. How had he died? I wondered. What would she say? What excuse would she make up this time? I knew it. I just knew it, that yet again she'd wielded her axe to score a hat trick. But how had she managed to pull it off?

"Hello," her frail voice sounded down the line.

"Mother! It's me."

"Oh, Billy, thank God! I've been going through hell. Stan died yesterday and it's hit me very hard. I can't cope anymore. Darling, can you come home and manage things for me?"

"Sorry, darling, but no. The show must go on and all that. You be strong now, Mother, you know you are really. I won't be able to be with you till Sunday. Try and fix the funeral for next Monday morning. That'll allow me time to travel to Leeds on the Monday afternoon for the show on Monday night. I'm playing there next week."

"Oh, darling, can't you come really? I need you so. I'll never get through this on my own."

"Sorry, darling, that's showbiz. See you Sunday. You be strong now."

In deference to Stan, the pub was closed on Sunday. I arrived after lunch and Mother and I spent a strange day alone together. With weepy eyes, she sat in her armchair, the dogs as usual at her feet, explaining how it had all happened.

I listened, alternating with feelings of compassion for her, to suspicions that she was lying because she'd bumped him off.

"It was only last Sunday, a most heavenly sunny day, it was. I said to him after we'd closed the pub, 'We ought to go out for a picnic.' We set off in the car and found a perfect spot in a field outside Barham, a superb view. Well, you know how lovely it is out there. Anyway, we spread the rug out and, just as I was unpacking the tea things, Stan sat on a bee. Stung him, it did, right on the bottom! Oh, it was just terrible; he was in agony, poor man, such pain. I didn't know what to do. I managed to get him back into the car but, of course, he couldn't sit down. Wheezing and vomiting, he was, with the nausea lying on the back seat. His lips were all swollen. I could barely concentrate on the driving and the roads were packed, what with it being such a fine day. They had road works up on the A2, too, so it took forever. By the time I got him to The Chaucer hospital, it was too late. He'd gone. Oh, it just doesn't bear thinking about. What I suffered. What I went through. It nearly killed me. They called for an autopsy... here, I wrote it down." She opened her handbag to read what she'd written on a scrap of paper. "They called it 'Anaphylactic poisoning'. They said it was very rare. Only four people in a thousand are allergic to bee stings and my Stan had to be one of them."

At the funeral on Monday morning she forwent her usual veil, instead she wore a black velvet cloche which left her face clear, stark, white. With her tailored black coat, black leather gloves, black stockings and her tiny feet in the inevitable high-heels she looked like a neat mannequin doll. To my surprise she was quiet and vulnerable in the church; the steel in her temporarily stilled. There were no histrionics, although I was constantly prepared. I was by her side throughout; I left her only to read the lesson. Looking down from the lectern at her chic form in the pew, her great green eyes, still beautiful, clearly turned up to me, I wondered if she'd choose this moment for her breakdown. But she remained still, holding my gaze. Quite suddenly her expression changed. She smiled at me. It was a smile so sweet, so warm, so very loving, it took my breath away. It seemed to me it was the first time she'd ever given me such a dear smile. My eyes dropped to the text.

Swallowing hard to control my emotions and the lump in my throat, I started to read.

Ecclesiastes. Chapter Three. To everything there is a season, and a time to every purpose under the sun. My quavering voice echoed around the church. I was bewildered. My voice was usually strong, yet now... Why? I didn't love her. I'd never loved Stan. He was no more to me than a sawdust man who did Mother's bidding. Why was I feeling this way?

A time to be born...

I remembered crying for her as a little boy when I'd been fostered out to the woman who hit me with a stick. When she had sent me away, I reminded myself. Why had she sent me to those foster homes and the sanatorium? Why?

A time to build up. A time to weep and a time to laugh.

I hated the woman; she was quite probably a murderess... and yet I'd never given her away.

A time to mourn and a time to dance. A time to embrace, and a time to refrain from embracing.

The world attributed qualities of sincerity and love to her that long ago I'd perceived were as fictional as the publicity of a film star. 'It would have been better if you'd never been born,' she'd said.

A time for love and a time for hate.

A time of war, and a time of peace.

I looked up at the congregation, my eyes met Mother's.

Dry-eyed she gazed back. Had she guessed how I despised her?

I closed the Bible and returned to her side. Her gloved hand squeezed mine.

Despite myself my tears fell.

As the mourners lined up to offer her their condolences after the ceremony, she wept. I didn't believe she was acting. Was a sliver of clemency creeping into my soul? Or was it that I needed her love? As I see it now, that was the most likely, for, though I was in my twenties, I was still a kid in a man's body.

I looked up 'anaphylactic' in the dictionary; it said, "Exaggerated allergic reaction to a foreign protein resulting from previous exposure to it." To me, at the time, dying from a bee sting seemed pretty implausible. I know now it's possible, but then, it seemed most unlikely. Could she have killed again? If so, how, and why? Was it anger at his affair with the barmaid? Maybe she'd injected him with some sort of venom? Or knowing he had this aversion, maybe she'd captured a bee in a jam jar, shaken it like a cocktail shaker to make the bee angry then released it after dabbing honey or pollen onto his jacket. No, no, my imagination was going into overdrive. One thing was clear, if she'd reached the hospital earlier his life would certainly have been saved, and later on she undoubtedly changed her tune about him.

Two months after his funeral, she invited me to stay for the week-end to help her clear his clothes out from his wardrobe in their bedroom. "Bless you for coming, Billy," she said. "I couldn't face doing this alone."

But she was not exactly overcome with grief as she crossly flung his suits and shirts into a trunk. With a good deal of asperity, she told me the following story.

"I didn't tell you before, but in the hospital after Stan died, the matron gave me a paper bag with his clothes in and an envelope. The envelope contained his signet ring, his wristwatch and wallet. In his wallet I found this." From her handbag she produced a dog-eared snapshot of a girl of about sixteen standing in a suburban garden.

"Whoever is this?" I asked.

"I had no idea. I had it over there by my mirror for ages." She indicated her kidney shaped dressing table by the window with a plate-glass top, it had a pretty floral skirt in the matching pattern of the bedroom curtains. "I stared at it for weeks wondering. Trying to puzzle out who she was and wondering why he'd kept it. Then the other day a letter arrived addressed to him. I opened it. 'Dear Dad,' it said. It was signed 'your loving daughter Marjorie'. It was this girl asking him why the cheque hadn't arrived." She flourished the photo in my face. "This was Marjorie, asking him if he could spare some cash."

Mother glowered with fury.

"All those years we'd been married, twenty-three years, he'd been lying to me. It was this girl here in the snapshot. His filthy, bloody illegitimate daughter by god knows who. The dirty filthy..." Words failed her. Ferociously she tore the snap up into tiny pieces and disguarded it in the dustbin.

"But Mother, aren't you curious at all to meet her?"

"I certainly am not! She can rot in hell as far as I'm concerned." Her nostrils flared and her scarlet lips pursed with rage; she wiped them angrily with her handkerchief and I glimpsed the steel she was made of and the mother I recognised. "That helped me get over the bastard's death."

That and her love of funerals.

For it was at yet another one that she met husband number three, for Mother was never one to be without a man for long.

Chapter Thirteen

Falling in Love Again

1961-1962

Why had I never given her away? Did my silence make me an accessory? Even after Stan's death, I still never said anything. But then no one else questioned his death, everyone seemed to accept it as quite normal that he should die from a bee sting. Why had I never at least confided in someone? Maybe I should have gone to a shrink? At this point in my life I certainly needed help to straighten out my sexuality. Of course I never had any proof Mother was a murderess, maybe I'd remembered it all wrong, maybe I'd imagined it, maybe I'd just got the wrong end of the stick.

Three months after Stan died she sold 'The Olive Branch' – for he left everything to her in his Will – and with the profits bought, and proceeded to transform, two dilapidated 18th century workmen's cottages in Barham into a three-bedroom, 'Country Life' type show home. Two months later, after completing it, she heard that a lady who had once fostered me, had died. "I really should go to her funeral," she declared, "but I couldn't possibly. It would be too upsetting."

Naturally she went.

Driving across three counties to the appointed church in the village of Hassocks in Sussex, she re-met the grieving widower, Joe Walsh, a retired builder. Now in his late seventies, he was lonely and inconsolable. After the mourners left, Mother stayed on to cook him supper. They shared old friends, mutual experiences, and, most important of all, they remembered those far-off days before their world turned lax and sour. Three months later she was still there.

"What would you say," she asked me coquettishly over Sunday breakfast at her Barham cottage, "if I were to get married again?"

"Wonderful, Mother, congratulations. I think it's a grand idea."

Her flirtatious expression abruptly dropped. "Wouldn't you be jealous at all?"

"Certainly not, why on earth should I be?"

"Oh! I rather thought you would be." She was clearly disappointed. During the morning she pottered about, musing aloud, giving me little hints as to her state of mind – in truth she was pulling my strings, jerking me into showing signs of emotional life. "Should I go to Hassocks to live with him permanently? Or..." she sighed heavily, "he so loves this little shanty of mine. But if he lived here he'd miss his own home. He's turned his cellar there into a workshop. He's so wonderful with his hands; he made that letter rack by the desk over there. Pretty, isn't it? Of course I'd still keep on the cottage, I'd never want to sell this, but then...if something were to happen to me..."

I fell into her trap, as I always did. "Perhaps my name could be added to the Deeds of the cottage to cover whatever might transpire," I said, and to demonstrate my prudence in matters legal, added, "to avoid death duties?"

"So now, it's out." All subterfuge was suddenly dropped. She snapped into focus and glared at me ferociously. "Money! That's all you've ever been interested in. My money." She took flight a la Crawford, Davis, and an aggrieved Greer Garson all rolled into one. "Never mind about me! Never mind about my happiness. You don't care a fig if I'm lonely and miserable living here on my own half the time."

No, she was right there.

"You're jealous, jealous of my happiness, that's what you are. Just because your own life is in such a mess, you just can't bear me to see me happy, can you?"

Her habit of always asking rhetorical questions drove me crackers. No matter what I said she was obdurate and refused to discuss the matter rationally. All because at breakfast I'd not answered: "No, Mother, don't marry again. Another man must never come between us," but I could no more have uttered such hornswoggle as play Hamlet in Japanese.

This slip of mine strengthened my resolve to keep her out of my life. She only ever upset me and gave me aggravation, what was the point? However, she did make me laugh. Trying to placate her I said, "I'd be really happy if you were to marry again, Mother. Honestly I would. You obviously get on well with him. Do you, um... sleep together?"

"Good heavens, no," she said. "I'll have nothing more to do with him if he starts growing big in front!"

I guess Joe never did grow 'big in front' because two months later they were married in Hassocks Registry Office. I didn't go to the ceremony because, by then, I was working up in Birmingham, where, I confess, I was growing rather big in front myself.

The object of my passion this time was the actress /dancer playing the Fairy Queen in *Mother Goose*. It was Panto time and I'd been engaged to play 'King Rat'. I was thrilled at the prospect for I'd never been in a pantomime before. I had to make my entrance through a trap door in a flash of green smoke wearing a sparkly blue crew-cut wig, a princely dress coat with a great stand-up green sequined collar and dark green tights. Best of all I had to dance. Well, actually leap about to the music of Franz Lehar's 'Gold and Silver Waltz' in a kind of *Swan Lake* pastiche. I ran around the stage with a great cloak billowing behind me trying to stop the Fairy Queen from turning Mother Goose into a swan. I'll call her Jeannie, not her real name, because she later became very famous. She was, and still is, a honey, just gorgeous; the sight of her in her glittering tutu drove me nuts. My digs were close to the theatre and we did 'the business' there regularly, well, pretty near everywhere, actually; in the dressing room between shows, almost in the wings, we couldn't keep our hands off each other. Our sequined bodies were drawn to each other like electro magnets and could barely be parted, sparks and sequins flew everywhere. The manager of the theatre, who was an old queen who'd made it very plain he'd taken a shine to me, was most put-out. "What would the children think," he wailed, clasping his fingers to his pink cheeks, "if they knew the Fairy Queen was being rogered rigid by the Demon King every matinee?"

I don't know where we got our energy. Any doubts I'd had about which side of the fence I was, vanished. Those legs of hers were so supple they went everywhere, higher and wider than anyone I'd ever been to bed with.

The show inevitably closed and we both sadly went our separate ways, Jeannie into a new musical that was to make her a star, me up to the Scottish Highlands, where I'd been engaged as leading man in a season of six plays at the Pitlochry Festival Theatre. This change of gender as the object of my passion surprised some of my friends but delighted me. Not that it had been a pretended passion, far from it; my lust for Jeannie had been only too earthy. Maybe I was growing out of homosexuality, I thought, maybe I was maturing; anyway Jeannie had certainly made me feel good about myself once again.

I clocked Annie on the first day of rehearsal, thinking she was the prettiest girl I'd ever laid eyes on. She looked like Snow White with her peachy complexion and black hair – subsequently I discovered it was dyed. I said to myself, I'll learn the lines first and then get around to you. She was a classy girl of twenty with the pneumatic figure of a page-three girl. Later I learned she was the daughter of a naval officer.

I became more and more aware of her presence during rehearsals and started looking forward to the scene in one play when we had to embrace. At the last rehearsal she parted her lips a little and, for a moment, I came out of character and sipped a taste of heaven. At the dress rehearsal, as I watched her from the stalls, I couldn't stop myself grinning. She looked so pretty, dressed in a huge pink crinoline, I thought she should be put on a teapot and used as a tea cosy. I promised myself, lecherously, that after the first night I'd see more of her and bundle her up into my bed.

A fortnight later, to my great joy, we were living together. Annie brought me rapture, exaltation, laughter and tenderness, and I could think of little else. That summer was a time of enchantment for me. I was playing superb parts in a season of successful plays and I was in love, and, wonder of wonders, she had spoken those three all-important words to me. After eight months of living in Eden, the end of our contract was in sight, but I couldn't bear the thought of parting from her. It cannot end here, I thought.

One night after the performance I wandered thoughtfully in the moonlight beside the trickling burn that ran through the woods near our apartment. That I had found my heart and loved Annie, I had no doubt anywhere, she combined sweetness and strength, a beauty and talent that was irresistible. But marriage? I'd never thought such a thing possible. Were my feelings strong enough to turn me into a faithful husband? Could I settle down, could I put a stop to my libidinous life style, my desire to sleep with men? I was thirty at the time and thought I was fully formed. I remembered my time as a choir boy and my Sunday school scripture lessons, Paul of Tarsus' letter to the Corinthians in the Bible. "When

I was a child I spake as a child, I understood as a child; but when I became a man I put away childish things."

Now that I was a man my answer to myself was a resounding, 'Yes'.

Later that night I asked Annie to marry me.

Joe drove Mother up to Scotland to see the plays and to meet her.

Mother was proud of my thespian achievements with the limited proviso that I played a 'nice' part. This was more complicated than it sounds. 'Nice' parts were not necessarily leading parts, not even good parts. If the part was 'not nice', i.e. was below stairs, didn't wear a suit, chewed gum, was a crook, had long hair, I would fail to win her approval. I could fool her if I dressed well, or smiled as I played the villain, which was fine for 'Raffles' types, but did not work for 'Iago'. Well, he was but a common sergeant, never mind that he had more lines to say than Othello. In this season of plays, however, I was playing some very 'nice' parts.

Introducing Mother to Annie after the show, I was mindful of her criticisms of my previous girlfriends – "she reeks of B.O." and "her hands are like hams" – and of my gay confession – only four years ago. As Mother scrutinized Annie, I watched hypnotized, thinking it was a bit like the Wicked Queen meeting Snow White.

"You're so beautiful," said Mother, digging her scarlet talons into Annie's carefully coiffed hair, "I could eat you up. I've always longed for a daughter and you are she. I love you to bits already."

The trouble was that Annie didn't much care for Mother; she called her a control freak and blamed her for my 'confused' sexuality, for I'd been quite open with her about my past. As Annie had about hers; she confessed to me that she'd had an abortion when she was eighteen while at the R.A.D.A. This rather knocked me back somewhat, for she appeared to be the very epitome of pink and white virginity, but as she forgave me my past, so I had to hers. We are both adults, I thought, the past is dead. We're in love and starting a new life together. I did not confide to her my belief that my mother was a murderer; perhaps because I had begun to think I'd invented the whole thing and was unsure, perhaps because I considered the whole unholy thought even more sacrosanct than my sexuality, anyhow I remained silent on that subject, and always have done.

At our Wedding Reception at Stratford-on-Avon, where Annie's parents lived, we were lining up to greet the guests when I noticed Mother and Joe were absent. My Best Man was my architect chum that I'd sailed up the Thames with when I was at drama school. "Charlie," I hissed, "where's Mother?"

An expression of utter horror crossed his face. "Oh, my God!"

"What is it?"

"I left her at the church. She was having her picture taken with the vicar."

"But she doesn't know the way," I said.

Charlie fled.

She was left waiting at the church for over half an hour before he collected her; something for which Charlie never forgave himself, and for which Mother never forgave him. She eventually arrived in a fury, her great vermillion feathered hat trembling with wrath, she glared at the guests and at the sumptuous spread my in-laws had provided with the critical expression of a livid, sneering Madame Guillotine; later, though, after a few gins, she revived enough to give Annie and me some advice.

We were fooling around in the kitchen when she came in and caught my wrist in a vice-like grip. "Shut the door," she demanded.

I obeyed, wondering what the hell was coming.

"Right, now we're alone I want to say something. Glasses up," she ordered, topping up our champagne glasses. "Now listen to me. This is important. Just between the three of us. I've been married three times and I have to tell you this. There'll be times when you'll hate the sight of one another. You'll want to commit murder."

Annie gave a sudden yelp of laughter, but as sure as hell, I didn't.

"Don't laugh," Mother reprimanded, "there will be, believe you me. You'll want to kill him, kill each other, I know. But be happy. Stick in there. Cheers!"

Anne pulled a face and giggled as we drank the toast, but at the back of my mind it occurred to me that, with two husbands down and a third in hand, so to speak, did this mean Joe was next in the firing line? Should I warn him? What on earth would I say?

An hour later feeling very happy, full of hope and excitement, we drove away on our honeymoon.

Annie had had her heart set on Venice. I had tried to change her mind with suggestions of sunnier climes, the Maldives or the Canary Islands, but no, she was adamant. "Venice is the most romantic place in the world," she pined.

"It won't be in December," I'd answered. "We'll be wrapped up in scarves and have to wear thermals."

"Oh, darling, please. I know you've been there before but it's been a childhood dream of mine to go to Venice with the man I love. We must go, please. We'll be tucked up in bed most of the time, anyway."

I was as putty and so in love with her I'd have taken her to Timbuktu had she asked. Ten years had passed since my fling with Giovanni, and he had most definitely not featured in our mutual confessions session. Hearing that her groom had once had a zonking great affair with a gondolier in her dream honeymoon resort was not, I judged, among the list of things a young bride wished to hear. So I'd kept silent and took pains to book a hotel as far away from Miss Guggenheim's Palazzo Venier dei Leoni as I could find. I'd heard that Miss Guggenheim had since become an Honorary Citizen of Venice but had no plans to renew our acquaintance. I was, of course, mildly curious to know if Giovanni still lived and worked there, but I didn't want to run the risk of bumping into him if he did. Though, I admit, when I saw the rows of gondoliers standing by their gondolas waiting to be hired lining the canals, I did wonder if Giovanni might be among them. Mercifully he was not.

Annie and I spent the most blissful two weeks ever. When we did venture out of bed, I was able to show her, like an experienced traveller, the islands of Torcello, Borano, and Morano – where we watched a miniature swan being fashioned for us at the glassworks – visit the Basilica di San Marco, the Palazzo Ducal and even go to some of the same restaurants that Norman had taken me. There was no 'nostalgia de Giovanni' whatsoever, for that clandestine affair seemed very long ago and far away, anyway it had been conducted strictly behind closed doors, so I'd only ever seen Venice proper with Norman.

All was wonderful until our penultimate day. It was a warm and sunny afternoon so we took a vaporetto across the lagoon to the Lido. Once there we strolled carefree, hand in hand, as lovers do, along the sandy beach paddling in the surf. We talked of our plans, kicking up the sand and chasing each other, until, reaching a hotel terrace we decided to sit and have some tea. We ordered and waited, idly watching an attractive young couple playing tennis on the hotel courts beside us.

Suddenly, in a freak shot, their ball flew over the wire netting and headed towards us, bouncing and coming to a standstill nearby. I rescued the tennis ball and, moving nearer to the court, threw it back over the wire mesh. The man in white shorts picked it up and nodded his thanks to me, but, as he looked, he halted in his tracks, as did I. It was Giovanni. His thick black hair hung over his brows, his lips parted in astonishment as he moved hypnotised towards me. I, in turn, moved closer to the wire.

Staring at me he whispered, "Billy?"

I smiled back, looking straight into his intense black eyes. "Giovanni."

His eyes shifted focus to Annie sitting at the table behind me. "Molte grazie," he muttered, moving swiftly away to continue his game.

It was clear he wished to forget what had once been. As indeed did I.

In London it was the time of the so-called swinging sixties. Beatles music was playing on the wireless, Twiggy's photo was on the front of magazines, *Hair* was playing at the Shaftesbury, and I was lucky enough to be offered an excellent supporting role in a big international movie. The director had once been an actor I'd worked with in Carlisle rep years ago, he remembered me and, after a film test, gave me the part. It eventually became a top grossing movie and was awarded three Oscars. With the money I earned I bought our house in Parson's Green, I put in central heating, decorated it from top to bottom, and it was from there eighteen months later I rushed Annie to hospital for the birth of our first daughter, Rebecca. Standing beside Annie, her hand gripping mine as she gave birth, was the most miraculous experience of my life and, as I held my daughter in my arms for the first time, I swore an oath. I promised I'd do everything in my power to ensure she had a happier childhood than I'd had.

When Annie came out of hospital, Mother invited us for the weekend to her cottage. "I'm just dying to meet my new granddaughter," she cooed down the telephone.

The following Friday afternoon, my senses heavy with dread, I drove us down to Barham.

Chapter Fourteen

Family Weekend

1962-1972

As we arrived Mother and Joe came out of the cottage to greet us. Annie got out of the car first while I retrieved the baby in the carrycot from the back seat. Mother immediately collected Rebecca up in her arms and without a grain of humour said, "Now leave the little darling with me. You two can go back to London."

I laughed nervously but Annie answered coolly, "No, we won't do that Vi. She's doesn't know you. Anyway she's not a doll you can just pick up and play with."

That rather set the tone for their future relationship.

I spent the entire weekend treading on eggshells, aware the two women in my life did not care one jot for each other, and, what's more, had no intention of trying to rise above it.

Never once did Mother mention my Oscar-winning movie, though at the time everyone I met wanted to talk about nothing else. The nearest she came to acknowledging its existence was a remark about one of its stars; "That Dirk Bogarde seems a very nice sort of man. I wonder why he's never married."

I could have told her, but Dirk had been exceedingly pleasant to me, so I kept my council. Squinting comically at Annie, I answered, "He's married to his art."

By the time Sunday afternoon came around it was time to leave. I was a nervous wreck and mighty relieved it was all over....but of course it wasn't.

Mother never came up to London to visit us in the home we were so proud of.

"What, come up to that filthy place? Not on your life. It's not the same as it was in my day. I hear they've even done away with the clock at Victoria Station!"

Two years later Annie was pregnant again. When we told Mother on the phone she was thrilled, and invited us for another weekend. Rebecca was, by now, walking and creating havoc wherever she went and Mother's cottage was not, I recalled, toddler-proof. In the car driving down for that damned weekend, I warned Annie, "We must watch Becky doesn't play with any of Mother's precious ornaments."

Mother was such a demon for perfection I suspect she suffered from what physiotherapists now call N.P.D – narcissistic personality disorder – apparently not uncommon among women who survived the Second World War and who frequented the cinema in the days of the high-glamour stars. Mesdames Dietrich, Garson, Stanwyck, and of course, Bette and Joan had a lot to answer for. Those perfectly-lit alluring goddesses, whose images were moulded, gowned and groomed by the slickest professionals in the world, were not meant to reflect reality, they were fantasies on which the public could project their desires. Mother never understood that, she longed to be all of them. They, or rather their images, were the most important influences in her life, more so than any cataclysmic event some analyst might unearth from her childhood. At the dining table in Mother's house, I often thought it was more important to her that her hair was done, the flowers were fresh, and salt and pepper correctly placed, than that there was a good flow of conversation.

On that fatal Sunday morning I was lying on my bed reading a book when Mother walked in, furious. "Oh, here you are! What do you think you're doing in bed at ten o'clock in the morning?"

"I'm not in bed. I'm on the bed having a pause."

"Don't be facetious with me, my boy, and get your shoes of that counterpane." She knocked them to the ground, making me feel I was a child of eight-years-old again.

"I was reading, Mother."

"There's a time and a place for everything and it's not in the morning. You will please get off that bed. Tell your wife to clean up the mess in the kitchen, put things away where they belong, and apologise."

"Why? Whatever has she done?"

She turned away muttering, "I've never heard of such a thing, a fine way to bring up children, I must say."

"Why? What has she done?" I insisted, following her.

"I don't want to talk about it."

"What has she done?"

"Do as I ask, please," was her only comment as she went down the stairs.

At the top of the stairs I lost it. "What has she bloody well done?"

She turned with eyes blazing. "Don't you dare shout at me."

"What on earth's the matter, Mother?"

"There's nothing the matter with me. This whole weekend you've deliberately tried to aggravate me. You come down here in those filthy jeans, your hair all over the place. You don't even have the common or garden courtesy to get up in the morning to eat the breakfast I cook."

"I never eat breakfast."

"It's the first I've heard of it. It used to be your favourite meal."

"When I was a boy, Mother, when I was a boy."

"You still are. Sniggering behind my back, the pair of you, I've just about had enough."

"Look, I didn't come down here for all this."

"Do you think I'm enjoying it? That counterpane was only washed last week."

"For God's sake, what's a counterpane got to do with it?"

"I washed it especially for you."

"Well, thank you. I was enjoying lying on it!" I grinned at her hoping she'd see the joke. "Mother, you have so much going for you, so much ...vitality, why do you waste it on trivia?"

"You think you're so clever, don't you? When in Rome, my boy. When in Rome. I like to keep my house decent."

"What the hell does it matter if the fucking counterpane gets dirty? Things do not matter. We are more important than things."

"Don't you dare speak to me like that." Taking a deep breath she added, "I am deeply upset. I'm going into the garden for some fresh air. You will please clear up that mess in the kitchen and ask Annie to apologise."

Downstairs my baby daughter was sitting on the kitchen floor bashing a row of saucepans filled with water as if she were Ringo Starr. Annie was perched on a stool grinning at her. "Do look," she said as I came in, "she's having a whale of a time." Then, as she caught my expression, added, "Oh dear! Was that shouting about me?"

"What happened?" I asked.

"Your mother found her playing with these pans and hit her. I told her not to."

"What?" I cried. "We're leaving!"

"We can't."

"We can. She wants you to apologise, if you please! You get the carrycot. I'll clear up this lot."

Annie pulled a wry face and raised her eyebrows. "I don't mind apologising if it'll make things better, but what is this craziness going on between the two of you?" With a resigned shrug she added, "Do you know, I thought this might happen. But you're the boss. If this is what you want, we'll go. I'd better clear up this first."

"I'll do it. You go upstairs and pack."

As Annie left, Mother came and stood in the doorway watching me.

"It's alright, Mother," I said. "We'll leave. You can have complete tidiness for the rest of the weekend. I know you'd rather have that than all of us being happy together."

"You're being absurd. You don't have to be so melodramatic."

"That, Mother," I said, "is a case of the pot calling the kettle black." Sulkily I cleared away the mess, then, brushing past her went upstairs. Five minutes later Annie, Becky and I were packed-up and sitting in the car. Without kissing Mother or even saying goodbye to her I drove away knowing I'd behaved badly, yet feeling relieved.

As I looked back in the driving mirror, I could see her standing by the garden gate watching us.

"I'm proud you stood up to her," said Annie, with her hand on my knee.

I hadn't stood up to her at all, though I was glad Annie thought I had. I'd just run away.

That, with a couple of half-hearted attempts at reconciliation, was the trifle our ten-year silence was based upon. At first I was embarrassed over the incident, telling myself family feuds have been built on lesser trivialities, but then came to realise that it was not the real reason, it was just an excuse. The real reason was buried deep in my subconscious, tucked away thirty years ago under my father's bed.

The immediate upshot was that there was no contact with Mother for six months. Then our son James was born. We knew we should tell her, but how? We weren't even talking. Eventually we wrote inviting her to the christening.

Two days later she telephoned. Annie answered.

"About the christening," said Mother. "I'll only come up providing I can bring James back here for some descent fresh air. Just the two of us, I can enjoy being a grandmother."

"But he doesn't know you," said Annie. Silently, but with her lips pressed, Annie passed the phone over to me.

"If your wife won't allow me to bring James back, what can I say?" said Mother. "There's really no point in my coming up." The phone went dead.

So the silence continued... for a further six years.

Mother's tiny eldest sister, Evelyn came to James's christening, but, on arrival said, "For Heaven's sake don't tell your mother I was here, she'll never forgive me."

Christmases and birthdays were cordially observed but otherwise the silence was a blessed relief.

Meanwhile my career wasn't doing too badly. I did a couple of goodish films and my first proper West End play, at the Aldwych for the Royal Shakespeare Company, and the following year, one at the National Theatre at the Old Vic, but, as far as I knew Mother never came to see either.

Then, suddenly, my dear Uncle Ralph died. Barely able to speak, my Auntie 'Pop Goes Your Heart' told me her heartbreaking news on the telephone. "I've arranged for a cremation at Worthing Crematorium," she said. "Would you be able to read or saying something, darling?"

"Of course. I'll look something up and let you know."

As I searched through my poetry collection, looking for something suitable, I wondered if Mother would attend the funeral. I knew from Auntie 'Pop Goes Your Heart' that she had not seen her former brother-in-law for many years, but I also knew that

Mother loved funerals, especially one where there was the possibility of her having a scene – in this case, a scene with me.

When the dreaded day arrived, we parked the car and waited outside the chapel.

Annie said, "She's never seen you with a moustache. I wonder if she'll mention it?"

"Only to say it doesn't suit me," I grinned.

"Which it does," said Annie, kissing me.

I spotted her just as she was alighting from a limousine. She was alone; Joe had wisely decided to stay at home. Annie and I girded our loins and went over to greet her.

She cut us dead. She turned her face away from us and walked straight into the chapel.

Annie and I took our places beside 'Pop Goes Your Heart', and when I got up to read, I looked down at Mother full in the face. She avoided my eyes. At the wake afterwards, she did exactly the same, she refused to look at me or say one word to either of us; it was quite, quite horrible.

That was three-and-a-half years ago, the last time I'd seen her before receiving Joe's phone call.

Chapter Fifteen

Setting Off

1976

"And take these snaps with you," said Annie handing me a packet of photographs of Rebecca and James we'd taken the previous weekend. "She'll love to see her grandchildren."

I made a face.

"Now get a grip, you're a forty-five-year-old man. Don't be such a silly Billy," she said, wrapping her arms around me as we stood in the hall. "Go, build bridges. She cannot hurt you anymore. All you have to do is smile and be your own charming self. You have the children, and me." She gave me a kiss on the cheek and tucked a stray lock of blonde hair behind her ear – she'd been a bottle blonde now for many years, for playing glamour-siren roles had become her professional stock in trade – both our children had my colouring, i.e. English mouse.

Yes, my beautiful family; somehow, after all, I'd found true love and happiness with my darling Annie. Despite those early fears of mine of being unable to settle down and fifteen years of marriage, I'd never once cheated on her, although opportunities had come my way. But why, I'd thought, risk damaging something so very precious? I suppose I was one of that rare breed in show business – an actor who believed in the institution of marriage.

There had been a hiccup two years ago when I'd found a love letter from one of her leading men hidden in her bedside drawer. I'd happened on it quite by accident when returning some handkerchiefs I'd ironed. The letter made it pretty clear they had been to bed together. I knew enough about sex to know that one swallow did not a summer make...nevertheless I agonised about it, wondering how to deal with it, and fretted how deeply she was, and had been, involved. She had never indicated to me that anything was wrong, the play they had been in had come to an end, and, so I hoped, had their relationship. I decided to hold my tongue. Whatever had gone on in her head she had managed to solve it, so why, I thought, dig it up again and invite recriminations? So the matter was never spoken of between us. These days, a night never passes but I lay my head on my pillow and, looking across at her lovely face next to mine, thank my lucky stars I had the wisdom to keep my mouth shut and bless the day we'd met.

"Sorry for being such a neurotic old fart," I said, tucking the snaps into my breast pocket. "I have now taken the butch pills and promise to be adorable to the old boot."

Earlier that morning I'd telephoned Joe in hospital to tell him I was on my way. He told me he wasn't feeling too hot, but said he'd call Violet immediately to let her know, which I thought tactful of him; it would have been an awkward call for me to make.

Annie kissed me goodbye. "You drive carefully, now."

I picked up my bag. There was nothing for it but to go.

It was a beautiful sunny morning. Filling up at a petrol station I passed my credit card over the counter to the cashier. He was a good-looking Indian lad who, baring his white teeth into a grin, announced, "You're off the telly!"

I nodded and smiled in my charming modest way.

"My wife won't believe it when I tell her you come in. You sign an autograph, please?" He rummaged around for a piece of paper.

At least he'd said 'please', some of them don't even do that. I signed the credit slip, then his piece of paper.

He seemed delighted until he looked at my signature. "Billy

Bartlett?" he said frowning. "I thought you was 'Old Roly'."

"Yes. That's the character I play, but my name's actually Billy."

"Ah!" he grinned. "You're an actor, right?"

"Right," I answered, and fled. Such was my small fame.

It had been nearly two years since my old friend Julia Smith, who'd been a stage manager in my early 'fringe theatre days' with Norman Marshall had asked me to play 'Old Roly'. Over the years she'd become an important television producer. She had warned me that if I accepted her offer I would never be able to walk down the street in anonymity anymore; at the time I didn't believe her. I still couldn't get used to complete strangers coming up and behaving as though they knew me, and knew me well. I'd never realised before the depth of the audience's participation and involvement in a popular soap opera.

As soon as I was out of the London traffic and on the motorway I couldn't stop my thoughts drifting to the past, to the maybe murders, the maybe murderess, and why, exactly, Mother was as she was. I was so busy reliving that last weekend at Barham and her cutting me dead at Ralph's funeral that I nearly missed the turnoff to Hassocks, the B2116. I swerved quickly and the car behind me hooted. Annie would have raised her eyes to heaven and left it at that; Mother, who prided herself on once being an ambulance driver during the war, would have had a blue fit. She was the most dictatorial back-seat driver ever. As a little boy when I used to sit in the back of the car, she'd literally scream instructions at 'Pop' Stan. "You madman! You're going far too fast, slow down," or "Can't you go any quicker than this? Put your foot down for Heaven's sake! We'll never get there at this snail pace." I used to feel quite sorry for him as she told him how to drive and where to go. Well, at least I'd been spared that for the last few years. Oh dear, I'd soon be with her. I was becoming a tad nervous and curious to know how she was going to receive me.

Chapter Sixteen

The Meeting

1976

It had just turned midday by the time I reached Joe's house. It was a detached turn-of-the-century villa with a well-kept front garden and at the side a newish asphalt driveway that gave up to a garage. I parked the car on the verge of the lane outside and opened the picket gate. Damn! I've forgotten to bring her some flowers....too late now. Rambling roses were growing around the front door, but there didn't appear to be a bell, so I knocked. As I waited I silently repeat a mantra to quieten my nervous tummy. 'No drama. Stay cool. You've faced worse than this on first nights. Do not allow her to get your Y-fronts into a twist.'

A thin wispy-haired woman wearing an apron and an inquisitive expression answered the door. Immediately she beamed, "Yes, it is you. I'd recognise that face anywhere. Come on in, sir, do."

Alert and watchful, I entered. "You must be Mrs Chapman," I said. "Mr Walsh mentioned you'd be here."

"We've been expecting you," she said, and then lowering her voice to a conspiratorial whisper added, "She's waiting for you in the lounge." Bowing as if ushering me into a throne room, she pushed open a door to reveal Mother.

She sat resplendent, bolt upright in what might well have been a throne; actually it was a padded Victorian armchair. She turned her imperious gaze upon me. The first thing I thought was, she's spent longer than usual in front of her dressing-room mirror this morning. She was immaculately made-up and groomed to perfection. Sunlight from the French windows beamed a halo onto the tips of her salt-and-pepper hair which was brushed up into style and probably sprayed rigid with Elnett hairspray. She wore a ton of jewellery yet somehow didn't look vulgar. A triple row of pearls circled her throat, a diamond tanzanite flashed on her finger next to Joe's engagement and wedding ring; on her right hand a bold aquamarine cocktail ring, the same colour as her eyes, stuck out from among her eternity rings giving an encrusted armoured-glove effect to her wrinkled liver-spotted hands. Her 'natural' painted fingernails, gleaming like lacquered locusts, griped the upholstered arm of the chair. Gigantic pearl earrings emphasised her glistening aquamarine eyes that even now were drinking me in, staring, penetrating to the back of my skull, as if saying, Well, what have you got to say for yourself? Her lips were compressed, not quite pursed, but almost; it was clear she expected me to speak first.

Surprisingly I was glad to see her. I smiled and stepped into the room. "Hello, Mother. How are you?"

Mrs Chapman hovered behind me watching, I guess she knew something of our history.

Mother spoke, but not to me. "You may go now, Mrs Chapman. Thank you so much for waiting. You needn't come tomorrow now my son's here. He'll look after me."

Oh, would I?

Her great aquamarine orbs returned to examine me.

Mrs Chapman said, "Enjoy your weekend. See you Monday; pleasure meeting you, sir."

"Thank you, Mrs Chapman," I said, watching her leave.

Mother and I were alone. For a long moment we held each other's eyes. Gazing into the face I knew so well, I could see how much she'd aged and I recognised something else, pain. Though motionless, I could tell by the way her nostrils dilated she was keeping a tight rein on her emotions. I, too, sought to disguise my soul rising into my eyes. "You look wonderful, Mother," I said, bending to kiss her.

"Thank you, dear."

"It's been a long time."

The corners of her mouth twitched into a thin smile. "How are my grandchildren?" Her voice had a cutting upward inflection.

"They're fine." Prepared, I reached for the wallet with their photos. "I've brought you these." I crouched by her side and showed them. "This is Rebecca on her bicycle, and this is James by his tent in the garden."

Mother examined them in silence, and then murmured softly, "They're so beautiful."

I became aware a tear was trickling down her cheek. "All those birthdays and Christmases lost."

"Let's not have any dramatics, eh?" I said rising. "Joe said you needed looking after, but you look great to me."

She wiped the tear away and said, "I've been very ill. I'm getting over an operation on my spine and if Joe's going to be in hospital for any length of time, I'd be more comfortable in my own home with my own things around me. Could you take me there?"

"What? Drive you to Barham, you mean?"

"Yes."

A net of horror slowly enveloped me as the pith of what she was requesting penetrated. I've been told I have an expressive face, which is a useful asset in my trade, but experience has taught me it is somewhat transparent when it comes to revealing my true emotions. At this point, without my being aware of it, the prospect of a two-hour drive, chauffeuring this back-seat-driving harpy telling me how and where to go, must have reflected on my face, for the said harpy, who could always read me like a worn-out paperback, narrowed her eyes and asked, "What's the matter?"

"Nothing," I lied, quickly making my face expressionless.

"What sort of car do you drive now? Can I see it?"

"Yes, of course," I answered. "It's a Honda, a Honda Civic."

"Show me," she said, making to rise, "I want to see it."

"Mother..." I hesitated, "How about a drink first?"

"Oh, my dear, of course, you've had a long journey." She melted into the hostess – well, almost. "They're on the sideboard, do help yourself. If you want a beer, Joe keeps some in the fridge. Use the crystal glasses; I'll have a G and T. And bring me some water, but I don't want tap water. Bring the bottled water in the fridge and some ice. There's a lemon there, too, just one slice, please."

With her issuing orders we were on safer ground, but, I reflected, we wouldn't be if we were to be locked in a car journey for a couple of hours. I'd probably murder her – which I should have done years ago. While I fixed the drinks I asked, "How long is Joe likely to be in hospital?"

"I've no idea," she replied. "Oh, he makes me so mad. I told him not to go up that bloody tree, but he never listens, stubborn man. Hauled out the step ladder, he did. I couldn't stop him. I told him, 'You're eighty-two!' But, oh no, up he went. 'If you want it trimmed, my dear,' he says, 'then trimmed it will be.' He's such an obstinate man. Frightened me to death, he did, falling like that. His accident had nothing whatever to do with me."

As Mother could read me, so I could read her. For her to be so defensive I guessed what she was telling me was untrue. She'd sent him up that tree as sure as God made little apples...she was covering herself. If Joe dies, she was thinking, the world will not blame me for bumping him off.

I might, though. If I was right and she'd done in her first two husbands and got away with it, then why not this one? I made a mental note to check the step ladder in the garden shed tomorrow to see if she'd interfered with it. Maybe she'd loosened the bolts that kept the top rung in place. Maybe she'd been at the bottom holding it, then wobbled it and the poor fellow had lost his balance and toppled...hold on, steady, Billy, don't get carried away. Wondering about a possible motive, I glanced around the comfortably-furnished room trying to guess how wealthy Joe was. There was a large television set in the corner with the stand-by red light on. This must be the set on which Joe had told me this morning that he and Mother watched my soap. "We watch every single episode and we love it," he'd said, but what was the betting Mother would never mention it? I also noticed a photograph of a young man wearing a mortar-board and gown, on the sideboard.

"Who's this?" I asked.

"That's Joe's son, Keith, who is now my step-son. He lives in Kenya. He married a black woman. They came over and stayed here last month. Great fat arms she had; and two children. So, can you believe, I have two piccaninny grandchildren!"

"Mother!" I reprimanded.

"Well, it's true. You know, when I came round after this last operation the first thing I saw when I opened my eyes was this black nurse standing over me. I screamed blue murder. 'Take your hands off me,' I said. 'I'm not having you touch me.' Except, of course, I could barely shape the words, which I suppose was a mercy. I felt awful afterwards, but I just couldn't help it. It was instinctive. Well, I'm of a different era, I'm not used to all this integration or whatever it is they call it. And now God has given me two piccaninny grandchildren. So he's having a mighty good laugh at my expense, I daresay. Oh, these last two months have been a nightmare. This last operation nearly killed me. I nearly died, I did."

She pressed her lips together and glared at me as if it were my fault. I guessed she was curbing herself from reprimanding me for not having visited her in hospital. Sipping her gin and tonic she rambled on about her health, which I'd forgotten was one of her favourite topics. It was an infinite and boundless subject, a saga that never bored her. Having enjoyed bad health for many years, she was in danger of never talking about anything else. She explained that driving her own car now gave her so much pain she never used it, which was why she now needed my help.

"Can't you go by train?" I asked, naively.

"I don't do trains," she said. "You have to go all the way up to London then down again. They don't go cross-country, it's quite ridiculous!" She drained her gin and placed the glass on her side table. "Now, then, let's have a look at this here car of yours." She rose from her chair and, for the first time, stood up. It was only then I realised how fragile she'd become. She was wearing high-heeled Charles Jordan shoes in the matching cream of her figure-hugging cashmere dress, through which I thought I detected the outline of a corset. "Give me your arm," she asked.

I did, and together we walked down the garden path. "Mother, you're not wearing a corset are you? You surely don't need to, you're so slim."

"Oh, don't," she answered. "Can you see it? This cashmere is so fine it shows everything. My surgeon recommended I wear one after my slipped-disc operation, but this one's a real bugger, it has steel bones."

"Isn't that uncomfortable?"

"Very. Oh, this looks nice," she said peering inside my Honda. I manoeuvred her into the passenger seat.

"Yes, very comfortable. I like that hand grip up there. Yes, this will do admirably. You don't mind driving me home to Barham, do you, Billy? Don't look so worried, I know the way. I can tell you exactly which roads to take."

I bet you will. Oh, Lord! Why can't I say, 'No'?

That evening after supper I chose one of her favourite L.P.s 'This was Richard Tauber', to put on the turntable. As Mr Tauber launched into, 'You Are My Heart's Delight', I judged it the right moment to escape, for I had come up with a plan. I'd made up my mind to leave, then to write her a letter suggesting she take a taxi to Barham. A coward's way, I admit, but I'd vowed not to have a row with her, which I surely would have if I drove her. After all, the purpose of this visit was supposed to be 'reconciliation' and 'closure'. But what excuse could I use to leave? I could only think of the wheeze used in plays I've been in. Call Annie... which I'd have to do from the village pub... ask her to ring here and say the studio needed me. This was before mobile phones, remember. I was just about to excuse myself – 'Popping down to the pub for some cigarettes' – when I became aware Mother was studying me. I turned to her, hoping she'd not read my sneaky thoughts.

With a mawkish look in her eye she said, "I was just thinking, now that your hair is going grey, your father would have looked just like you had he lived."

My hair wasn't going that grey. I was quite put-out. But then, she always knew which buttons of mine to press.

"Him, it would have suited." She sounded just like some Jewish mamma in a movie. "I'm not sure about the moustache though. Is it for your part in that television thing?"

"Yes, dear." Thing...thing? Don't rise to her, don't.

"You know you've always looked exactly like him, don't you? It's uncanny. He was the love of my life, that man."

In that case why did you kill him? I dared myself to ask.

"He broke my heart."

That might have been a reason. "You're happy now with Joe though, aren't you, Mother?"

"Oh, he's a sweet enough man and he thinks the world of me, but I don't love him. Not in the way I loved your father. Or even Stan. Oh dear, those last years with Stan...all he ever did was sit around in the afternoons watching the gee-gees on television, making bets with bookmakers on the telephone. He nearly lost us a fortune, you know. I had to put a stop to that." (And did you? I nearly asked.) "No, I married Joe because I was lonely. As you will discover when you grow older, being with someone is better that being alone. Loneliness is like a big black pain when you get to my age."

Perhaps it was the schmaltzy music that was making her so guileless; she was certainly being as candid as I've ever known her. Could I be the same, I wondered. Yes, I decided. "Mother, wouldn't you like to stay here in Hassocks so you can be near Joe and visit him in hospital?"

"Not on your life!" Her candor abruptly changed to naked self-interest. "I've had enough of hospitals these last eighteen months to last me a lifetime. I told him as much as they took him away. I said to him, I said, 'Don't think I'm coming to see you in hospital, because I won't.' Dreadful places. If he goes, then he goes; it's the last I'll ever see of the man!"

What a frightful woman you are, I thought. "Mother, I have decided not to drive you home tomorrow." The words popped from my mouth surprising even me.

She looked at me astonished. "What did you say?"

The Viennese charmer on the radiogram was lyrically imploring us to 'whisper I love you' into his ear.

"Turn off that row," she ordered.

Oops! Even Richard Tauber wasn't safe. Maybe I'd better get out now before things got worse? I stopped the record and in the silence said, "I'll pay for you to take a taxi, or even a private ambulance, if you'd prefer?"

"I'd prefer you to drive me home."

"No, Mother. We'd end up screaming at each other. It'll be much nicer for you if you have a proper chauffeur to drive you."

She looked me up and down and nodded. "Well, it's come to a pretty pass, I must say. My own son won't even take me home. How dare you?" she said, dangerously containing her fury. "After all I've done for you over the years. You think of nobody but yourself, you know that? You're a selfish little sod, you are. Get out! Go on, get out of my sight. I don't ever want to set eyes on you ever again. It was a mistake you ever coming."

Once more I experienced an overwhelming desire to wring her silly chicken neck. I placed my hands around her throat and pushed my thumbs onto her wrinkled throat. I squeezed hard. Harder. Throttle the bitch! "Mother," I said, controlling my fanciful imagination, "you have to remember that I was sitting in the back of the car all those years while you screamed abuse at Stan when I was a little boy. I know what you're like. I'm not going to allow you to do that to me. You'll have a much better journey in a comfortable taxi."

"It would cost a fortune," she sneered.

"I've told you, I'll pay."

"Oh, you will, my boy," she threatened. "You will. I'll see to that. Get out of my sight. "

I left immediately. It was almost the same situation as ten years ago, except, this time she did not come to the garden gate to watch me drive away.

Part Two

Chapter Seventeen

How Mother Got Home

1976

As I sit typing this on my laptop so many years after that event, I remember Mother loomed over my thoughts that night in 1976 like a monolith. I drove on through the dark trying to convince myself I'd done the right thing. Yet that was patently not so, for now we were in a worse predicament than ever. There was so much to think about, I couldn't think of anything. I did recall, though, that I'd not checked out the ladder, and wondered if I should nip back and do so. No, no, I answered myself, if she had persuaded Joe to go up that ladder in the first place, then she has to take responsibility for him falling off it.

My subconscious took over and things seemed to take shape within me. I sensed my emotions moving in the darkness, beneath the level of my attention and without my assistance. I loathed her yet I loved her. As a child, despite her dumping me in foster homes and putting me in that Institution, I'd always longed for her, believing myself to be loved. Somehow I knew it. But as I grew up, because of what I'd heard from under the bed, what I'd come to know of her, I no longer believed or trusted that love. She was acting, as she acted about everything. For her, life was a movie, a scenario in which she was the glamorous heroine, whereas I, as a working actor, was lost without a script to work on. In a play I knew exactly who I was and what to do, but in real life I was adrift, living and having to deal with people was much more difficult.

Both of us were influenced, I, more than I liked to admit, by what we'd seen on the movies. On this point our lives seemed to criss-cross, to intersect, like the spokes of a wheel. In public she'd act out her love for me, by pinching my cheeks, ruffling my hair and squeezing my ear lobes, announcing she could eat me up she loved me so much, but alone, in private, she'd either reprimand or ignore me. I had never known who she really was. So I'd forced myself to reject that public, affected mother-love, and determined never to seek her approbation. Instead I sought it of my peers in the theatre and my audiences. That's probably why I'd become an actor, to be loved and accepted, which is why applause was so important to me; why I went through life like some grinning apeth, trying, as an important director told me years ago, to please everyone and be loved. I'd had to work hard to eliminate that tiresome quality from my acting. All my relationships had seemed to flounder because I expected too much, all, that is, except Annie, who had given me so much joy and pride, as well as my two beautiful children. In a sense I'd poured all the love I'd denied Mother into her.

I turned on the car radio, it was Easy Listening. Headlights from oncoming cars blinded me but the more miles I put between us, the easier I became in my mind. I'd soon be home with Annie and the kids. Annie's career was now doing well, she was thirty-five and at the peak of her beauty. She'd become an excellent actress, having improved immeasurably since our days up in Pitlochry and I flattered myself I'd helped, for we always dis-cussed her roles in the minutest detail. She had a couple of televi-sion drama series under her belt and had twice been a leading lady in the West End. There had been an amusing incident during one of these productions when the designer had selected a dress for Annie she didn't like. She'd agreed to wear the dress for the tour providing that when the play came to London a new one would be forthcoming. Months later at the dress rehearsal in the West End,

Annie went on stage wearing the dress saying, "I was promised a new dress for this scene. Where is it, please?"

"You look divine in that one, darling," said the producer.

"I know how I look, thank you," she replied. "Where is it?"

"There will be no new dress," announced the producer. "We're over budget as it is. Continue please."

"In just one moment," said Annie disappearing into the loo.

She emerged five minutes later flourishing a large pair of scissors, wearing only a bra and a pair of cami-knickers. "The dress is now in shreds down the toilet," she announced. "So unless you're prepared to let me go on stage wearing this, then you'll have to buy me a new dress."

And of course they did.

"I want it all," she said to me one evening, "and why not? I want to be a wife, mother and have a successful acting career. Why shouldn't I?" With a good deal of juggling of the children and organization from both of us she was achieving her ambition.

I thought of my own career. Some career! I asked myself how much longer was I prepared to go on in the TV soap. Although I enjoyed playing my role, and it had certainly bought me popularity and a degree of celebrity, my first love had always been the theatre. Yes, I decided, I'll go back to the theatre where I can see the people and hear the applause.

It was three months later I heard the extraordinary tale of how Mother had reached her home in Barham. It was quite something. My Aunt Evelyn was giving me tea in her pretty chintzy apartment overlooking the Leas at Folkstone.

"There's not much you can tell me about my sister I don't know," she said, passing me a slice of Madeira cake on a plate. Evelyn, mother's savvy and astute elder sister, was now, astonishingly, coming up to her ninetieth birthday. She'd guessed, correctly, that I was reluctant to attend her birthday party if it meant bumping into Mother, who I'd not seen or heard from since driving away from Joe's house that night. "Remember, I've known her since she was a baby," she continued, "and, believe me, I know just what a monster she can be. I still love her, mind, but, oh, yes, the stories I could tell you about her and her boyfriends. But I'd best not go into that, 'cause I was probably just as bad!" And she puckered up her chin in a self-deprecating chuckle. "I want you to come to my birthday party," she insisted, "and don't you fret, your mother won't be here."

"But how do you know?" I asked.

"Because I'm the one who's going to be ninety, I'm going to be the star, aren't I? She won't be able to bear it. She'll pretend to be ill and stay away, you'll see."

I laughed. "It's such a relief to talk to someone else who sees through her. I thought I was the only one." Then, somewhat guiltily, I added, "I've not been in touch with her since Joe died."

"I know," said Evelyn, "she told me all about it." Our eyes met and she smiled. "When I didn't see you at his funeral, I guessed the way of things."

"Annie and I were in Italy. We didn't hear about it until we read the announcement in 'The Telegraph'."

"Joe left her everything, you know, in his Will; his house, all his investments, everything. Your mother will never want for a thing."

"I believe it," I said, wondering again if that's why she'd sent him up the tree.

"After you left that weekend she got on the telephone to your cousin Lizzy in Florida. She offered to pay her return air fare to Gatwick if she'd drive her home to Barham. Lizzy accepted. Well, she would, wouldn't she? I was waiting at the Barham cottage when they both arrived. I'd gone over to turn on the central heating and take her some groceries for the fridge. When the car turned in the drive I couldn't believe my eyes. Your mother was driving. She's had two bypass operations, a hip replacement, two new knees, fought off breast cancer and diabetes, she takes 40 different medications a day, has poor circulation, has hardly any feeling in her hands and feet, she can't remember if she's sixty-five or seventy-five, nearly all her friends have died, and there she was at the wheel! Next to her in the passenger seat was your cousin Lizzy sobbing her heart out, in a fine old state. Apparently y'mother had driven her so dotty during the journey criticising her driving, the poor girl had become hysterical. Well, the child had just flown four-and-a-half thousand miles across the Atlantic, probably without sleep, just to drive her majesty from Hassocks to Barham."

I grinned. "That might have been me."

"After I'd made us all a cup of tea, y'mother packed her off to Gatwick in a taxi and thence back to Florida, poor girl. So..." Evelyn wiped her lips with a paper napkin and muttered, "waste of blooming money, that all was. Would you like a nip of something stronger, dear?" she added, making for the sideboard and the brandy bottle. "Help us on a little, wouldn't it?"

"That would be grand," I answered. "Tell me, darling," I asked with a sigh. "Why is Mother as she is?"

Evelyn understood exactly what I'd meant, for a little smile hovered around her mouth as she poured the drinks. "That's a question and a half."

"You know her better than anyone," I added. "Why is she such a drama queen? What makes her tick? What was she like as a kid? You were there when she was growing up."

"Ah, but I wasn't," she said, handing me a small glass with a very large brandy inside. "Remember, I'm fourteen years older than she is. I left home just after she was born. But I know everything that went on, oh, yes, indeed I do." A shadow passed over her face. "I was there for her in the dark days, too." As if banish-

ing an unpleasant thought she flicked a quick smile at me.
"Cheers!" She sipped her brandy and her eyes twinkled as she
looked at me thoughtfully. "Maybe it's time you knew about those
days, too? It might help you understand her."

"Oh, Auntie," I said. "Do tell."

"You'll have to promise me you never heard any of it from me."

"I promise," I said.

"You want the long version or the short?"

"Oh, the long, Auntie, the long."

A faraway look came into her eye. She settled back in her armchair, patted her silver hair with an oddly comic primping gesture,
as if fortifying herself for the story ahead, and started to spill the
beans.

Chapter Eighteen

Eve's Story

1926

"At sixteen, Billy, your mother was just gorgeous. Truly. She, herself, was quite unaware of it, which, of course, made her even more attractive. One evening she turned up on my doorstep in the pouring rain.

'I've run away, Eve,' she says, looking like some drenched waif huddling in my doorway. 'Can I stay?'

I was married to my first husband, Len, at the time, and living in Paddington. I was working as a secretary to a Finance director in the City and had just arrived home. 'What on earth's happened?' I said. I was so shocked, I just stood there, holding up my umbrella, staring at her. Soaked to the skin, she was, wearing an old tam-o'-shanter, just a cardigan and a slip of a grey dress.

'I've been waiting ages,' she says. 'I didn't know where else to go. Promise you won't send me back, Eve?' She was such an innocent, with long auburn hair, heavy eyebrows and great thick eyelashes covered in raindrops. Mind you, she was wilful even then, but that evening, she looked very woebegone indeed.

'What about the children?' I asked, meaning our younger brother and sisters.

'I've left them to it. I've had enough, Eve. I want a life of me own.'

'You've done a bunk?' I said, astonished. 'You've left Cecil and the twins to fend for themselves? Does Muzz know?'

'She will by now if she's home from work, leastways I hope she does. She'll have to stay home and look after them herself for a change, won't she?'

Our mother, or Muzz, as we called her, worked at the Rothschild silk mill in Tring, near Aylesbury. She was a silk-hand twist worker and worked seventy-two hours a week. Our Dad was killed at the battle of the Somme back in 1916. With a family of eight mouths to feed, Muzz had become the breadwinner. After I left home, my two brothers took it in turns to look after the younger ones, after they left, Violet, as the next eldest, did the same. So she never had much of a childhood of her own, she seldom went to school and worked like a skivvy. She did the washing, the ironing, made the beds, cleaned the outside loo, the kitchen, went to market, fed the babies, everything. She took to it, too, which is perhaps why she's become such a demon of a housewife today. But that night it was a very different story.

'I'm sick of being a dogsbody,' she says. 'Being at everyone's beck and call, I've got ambitions for meself. I've been boiling up to this for ages, Eve. I want to make something of my life. I'm determined to and that's why I've left.'

'Let's get out of this rain for goodness sake,' I said, unlocking my front door and ushering her in. 'Len should be home soon. I can't say I blame you. It's a wonder to me you've stuck it as long as you have. I could never have done it. It's one of the reasons I left home when I did. But if Muzz stops work,' I muttered, putting my dripping umbrella into the stand, 'how on earth are they going to manage to keep body and soul together?'

'That's her worry,' she answers, her jaw set in that obstinate way of hers. 'Can I stay, Eve? I promise you I'll not be any trouble. I'm ever so tidy.'

'Of course you can, pet,' I said, thinking I'd have to send Muzz some cash out of my next week's wages. 'You'll have to make do on the sofa, mind, and it can only be for a short while, because Len works at home weekends.'

'Oh, Eve,' she gasps. 'Thanks. Thanks so much.' Then she lets go and sobs, more from relief than anything else, and I can see the strain she's under...it's been three or four hours since she snuck out of Muzz's home in Aylesbury and run to the station. She'd left Cecil in charge of the twelve-year-old twins telling them she was nipping to the shops, but she'd suffered agonies of guilt and worry in case of accidents or Muzz returning home late.

'First,' I say, taking off my coat and the new cloche hat I was so proud of, for they'd only just come into fashion then, 'we must send a telegram to Muzz telling her you're safe and staying here. She'll be worried sick. Get out of those wet clothes or you'll catch your death. Tomorrow, I'll take the morning off and we'll find you some work. How's your schooling?'

'I've not had much,' she says, wiping her nose and peeling off her clothes. 'I can read and write, but none too well. Cecil and me's been trying to teach ourselves writing from the books you left. But I do know how many beans make five, Eve. Me and my friend, Sylvia, went out dancing the other night and got chatting to the band leader. I told him I wanted to be a nightclub singer like Gertrude Lawrence, and he said he'd give me an audition if I could get meself to London and be at his club in Soho tomorrow morning. I've got his address here, look.'

Well, then, of course, the penny drops. 'I don't much like the sound of him,' I say, 'or Soho. Are you serious when you say you want to be a singer?'

'Of course.'

'Can you sing? I mean, really sing?'

'Of course!'

'Well, we'd better go and see the man, then. Let's hope he was serious.'

'Oh, he was, he was,' says Violet, all wide-eyed. 'He'd not have given me his address otherwise.'

'That's as maybe," I say, 'but I think I'd better come along too.'
And I did. The next morning we set off for the address in Soho.
Violet borrows one of my navy blue office dresses, for I've always
been small-boned and my dress size fitted her. Not perfectly,
mind, it didn't do much for her full girlish figure, if you know
what I mean. So she livens it up with these artificial violets she likes
pinning to her dress, her tam-o'-shanter and too much lipstick.

The address in Soho turns out to be a proper dive. A basement
with a sign, Private Club. My impression is of a red-light, disrep-
utable honky-tonk. It has striped regency wallpaper, red velvet
banquettes, miniature chandeliers, a dance floor and bar, where an
unshaven fellow in shirt-sleeves is stacking shelves. Chairs are
stacked up on the tables, and a harsh working light makes the place
look even shabbier and sleazier than no doubt it looked pinked up
at night. The place stinks of liquor.

'Well, well, if it isn't Shrinking Violet,' says this rather common
looking man in a broad shouldered bright blue suit, it turns out
he's the band leader, but in my opinion he's a greasy-haired smart
Alec. All smiles, he says, 'So you made it.' Looking at me side-
ways, he adds, 'Is this your school ma'am?'

'Yes,' I snap. 'I've come to ensure this is a bona fide audition.' I
felt perfectly justified at being so defensive for the place reeked of
sin. 'I'll make myself scarce at the back here,' I say, sitting down
feeling a bit of a prude, but my words do the trick, for his whole
demeanour alters.

'Please,' he says, 'make yourself at home.' Turning to Vi, he
rubs his hands, 'So, Violet, nice to see you again.' He introduces
the pianist. 'This is Morris.'

'What are you going to give us?' asks Morris, smirking.

'I don't have any music,' says Violet in her best voice, 'but do
you know "Look for the Silver Lining" from *Sally* by Jerome

Kern?'

Morris, by way of a reply, plays a flashy arpeggio finishing with an introduction to the song.

Violet gawps.

'Get up on the stage, honey,' says the band leader. 'In your own time.'

She shines her smile on him, as she does to every man she meets, though to give her her due she didn't realise the effect it had on a certain type of man in those days. She was completely unaffected then, but she learnt pretty damn quick. She'd muddle them all into a fever of lust in the next few years. Anyway, she walks to the centre of this little stage and starts singing the verse of the song... *Please don't be offended if I preach to you awhile...*

Now my musical experience at the time was not vast. I'd been to one or two Henry Wood promenade concerts at the Albert Hall. I knew I didn't care much for opera, but I did, and still do, enjoy a Gershwin or Cole Porter tune. I realised at once she was singing flat. The face on the pianist said it all, wincing in pain, he was.

The band leader bows his head, puts his hand through his hair and waits for her caterwauling to stop. 'Dear God!' he says. 'You have just murdered one of my favourite songs. Sorry, honey, but no. You will never ever have a career in singing.' He turns to me and says, 'Take her home, lady. Get her out of here. Teach her anything but not music. I'd be sued if I put her up on stage.'

'Why?' says Violet, trembling. 'What's wrong with me?'

'You really wanna know?' he asks with a dangerous look. 'Cause if you do, I'll tell you.'

'Tell me,' says Violet.

'You sing flat. You wave your arms like a windmill. You're coy and sentimental. You're a nice-looking girl, so I'll give you some advice. Grow up, give up any idea of singing for a living, and go find yourself a solid trade in Civvy Street. Good morning to you both.'

Vi was shattered. As we walked away nothing I could say cheered her up. That was the end of her life, or so she said.

Things didn't get much better either. Times were hard in the spring of 1926. She couldn't find any decently-paid work in London. The most she got was cleaning pots in a hotel.

'I'm worth more than this,' she says to me one night. 'I scrub and sweat over the sink in that smelly basement, but the pots just keep coming, they never stop. It's harder work even than it was at home.'

She stood it for two weeks, then left. Then she finds herself a job as a waitress in the Edgware Road, it's a cafe run by an Italian family. They were pleasant folk and she soon caught on that pleasing a customer resulted in a tip. If she flashed him her smile, the tip got bigger. I think that was when she started to learn something about people, about human nature. Well, as a waitress, I imagine you do. In May, a General Strike in support of the miners' claim for wages and hours was called, all the key industries in the country – railwaymen, steelworkers, and transport workers – came out in support. The strike lasted ten days and I had to walk back and forth to work every day.

It was about a month afterwards that she received the letter that was to change everything. The letter was from our mother's oldest sister, Alice White, who lived in Hove, it said:

> *Dear Violet,*
> *Your Mother has written to me expressing her anxiety about your situation.*
> *I have a dear friend in Hove, Mrs Bloom, who owns a millinery shop in Church Road. She tells me she needs someone lady-like and presentable to work behind the counter. I*

immediately thought of you. If such a post appeals, you would be most welcome to stay with us, we have a large house with plenty of rooms, and I'm perfectly sure Mrs Bloom would offer you the job if you presented yourself and made yourself available. Your cousins, Geoffrey and Bertie, have asked me to tell you they would be delighted if you came to stay, as indeed would I.

I know Eve and Len lead such busy working lives up in London it can't be much fun for a girl your age on your own. Do give them my love and tell them to come and see me soon.

Let me know your thoughts about this by return.

Love Aunt Alice.

Chapter Nineteen

The Flapper

1926–1937

Eve and Violet stood under the clock at Victoria station. I could just imagine them standing there as Eve was telling me the story – it played across my mind like an old black and white film. The clock said ten o'clock and a week had passed since they'd received Aunt Alice's letter. With Eve's help, Vi had penned an answer accepting the invitation; she'd given notice to the Italians, who were *molto triste* to see her go; now, here were the sisters, their eyes peering up scanning the train indicator. Violet's hair was coiled into a chignon and she was wearing one of Eve's navy blue office dresses, she looked just like a very young Joan Crawford playing the part of a salesgirl in one of her early movies; considerably more presentable than when she'd shown up on Eve's doorstep two months ago.

"Look," said Eve, "it says Hove, platform 15. You've got ten minutes. I'll say goodbye now, pet, 'cause I'm late for work as it is. God bless, and take care of yourself. And you mind your manners, make a good impression." She gave her sister a hug and kiss, knowing full well she was going into a very different milieu with Aunt Alice than she'd ever known before. "Give Auntie my love. Tell her I'll try and pop down to stay as soon as I can get away. You've got enough money for a taxi at the other end, haven't you?"

Violet nodded. "Mmm hmm."

"Take care. Love you. Bye." Eve made her way back to the bus stop, hoping her sister would win their aunt's approbation and not become downhearted at being the poor relation.

Violet stood alone holding the small suitcase Eve had given her, and watched till she was out of sight. *Now then, where's Platform 15?*

In Adelaide Crescent at Hove, she stepped out of the taxi and looked up in amazement at the great cream painted Regency house. *Golly! One, two, three, four, five floors, including the basement. I didn't know it was going to be this posh.*

She paid the cab driver – it was her very first time in a taxi – and feeling somewhat apprehensive mounted the three steps to press the polished brass doorbell.

A uniformed maidservant of middle years opened the front door. "Yes?"

"Hello! I'm Violet."

"Oh, please to come in, miss. Mrs White is waiting for you in the drawing room."

Violet stepped in onto the black and white marble chequered floor, gaping in awe at the entrance hall as large as a room. She saw a fireplace and above it, on the wall, a plaster of Paris escutcheon – the family crest of the late Colonel White. Vi didn't know what it was, she'd never seen such a thing before, but she was impressed, aware it represented majesty and might.

"This way, miss," said the maid, continuing up the staircase.

Violet followed her, passing framed prints of seascapes on the wall.

Stopping by an open door on the first floor, the maid said, "Miss Violet for you, Madam."

"Come in, come in, child," called a voice from inside.

Violet stood in the doorway. Before her was a magnificent room, large, airy and beautifully furnished. Her worn scuffed shoes sank into the thick rich carpet. There was a marble fireplace with flames licking up from the grate, over the mantel hung a brightly coloured oil painting of a vase of flowers. A fine collection of objects d'art was displayed in a glass fronted cabinet, and on various side tables stood silver bowls of flowers. Full-length swag velvet curtains hung either side of the balcony windows, framing the crescent gardens, across the road a lawn leading to the promenade, then the sea and vast blue sky. Seated at an elegant escritoire desk, smiling, but looking distinctly formidable, with sharp features and iron-grey hair, sat Aunt Alice.

Alice was a more sophisticated and well-to-do lady than Violet's mother, Muzz, having done rather better in the marriage market and wedded an officer and gentleman, but, like Vi's father, he, too, had died in the Great War. At first glance Alice looked as if she were a martinet, but Violet remembered Eve telling her that Alice's grey hair turned purple after a visit to the hairdresser. As a little girl Eve had thought it meant she was a witch, but a good witch, for Alice had a very warm heart. She had been born in the 1870s and still carried an air of the Edwardian era about her. She loved the scent of lavender, which she always wore, along with her long grey dresses, three rows of pearls and dangling marcasite earrings.

"Come here, child. Don't be shy, let me look at you."

Violet walked forward and stood before her aunt trying to smile.

"My!" she exclaimed. "You've grown into a very pretty girl." Alice took her chin in her hand and scrutinized her. "Good eyes. Excellent complexion. Is that Eve's dress you're wearing?"

"Yes."

"Very sensible. Exactly right for your interview with Mrs Bloom, which I have arranged for three o'clock this afternoon. We'll get you settled into your room. Have a bite to eat, I expect you're hungry, and then you can pop along to the appointment. It's only up the road. Your mother tells me you're good at maths. Mrs Bloom requires someone to manage the front desk while she creates her masterpieces in the workroom. Does being put in charge of a till hold any terrors for you?"

"No, I'd like it," answered Violet confidently. For from the age of ten she'd sat with her mother at the kitchen table every Friday night after the young ones had been put to bed and learnt how to balance the household accounts to the very last penny. 'Write down what is coming in and balance it against what is going out. If there is one penny going out needlessly, stop it, cancel it. Turning a profit, having money in your pocket, is the most important thing in the world and don't you ever forget it,' she'd impressed on her. 'Without money you're a nobody and will never amount to a thing. Money is like a force of nature. With it you have freedom to do what you want, without it you're nothing.'

"Splendid," said Aunt Alice. "Understanding finance is an essential in life, Beatrice!"

"Yes, madam?" replied the maid from the doorway.

"Take Miss Violet up to her room, then tell Saunders we will have luncheon." Addressing her niece, she instructed, "Run along now while I finish this letter," adding sotto voce, "Oh, and better give Beatrice those shoes to polish up. I'll see you in the dining room in ten minutes. You may give me a kiss."

Violet leant forward and kissed her aunt's cheek.

"Welcome to 'Belle Vue Sur La Mer'. You'll see your cousins this evening at dinner. Be off with you now."

At three o'clock precisely, Vi, her old shoes now polished a shiny black, presented herself at the millinery shop at 177A, Church Road. The shop door pinged as she opened it, and there, standing behind the counter stood a stout and homely, if slightly eccentric lady with an artificial rose in her hair. "I do believe this is Mrs White's niece," she postulated. "Good afternoon."

"Good afternoon. Yes," Vi answered shyly.

"But you are not wearing a hat."

"I hardly ever do."

"Well, we'll have to do something about that. You have just the correct shaped head for a cloche. What is your name?"

"Violet."

"Ah! Like the flower. Mine is Rose Bloom, which is why I always wear this in my hair?"

"Is it real?"

"Good heavens, no. This is an egret," she announced proudly. "It's my trade mark."

A fair-haired girl of a similar age to Vi hovered in the background. Mrs Bloom introduced her as "This is my assistant, Linda Thompson".

"Glad to meet you, Violet," said the girl grinning broadly.

Vi smiled back, warming to her immediately.

"Linda helps me in my workroom. Come, let me show you." Mrs Bloom lifted the counter flap with one hand and lead Vi behind the counter past the big brass Victorian till, into the inner sanctum.

Dominating the workroom was a large work table covered with padded white linen, a Singer sewing machine and boxes and boxes of pins. On the walls were shelves stacked with wooden hat blocks and felt hoods, small ones for cloches and wide-brimmed ones for picture hats; there were fine-woven straw hoods for bonnets, boaters, and bucket styles. There were dozens of hooks holding brightly-coloured ribbons, drawings and cut-outs from fashion magazines, pictures of elegant ladies wearing hats from Paris, London and Rome. There were cardboard boxes of feathers, rolls of lace and netting, and a gas ring with a steaming kettle for the shaping of felts where the subtlest curve of a brim could turn its wearer into a bewitching Delilah.

"I can offer you two pounds and ten shillings a week," said Mrs Bloom, after showing her the back entrance, the outhouse and where the dustbins were kept, "plus five per cent on every hat you sell. Is that satisfactory?"

"Very," answered Vi, thrilled at the prospect.

"Good. You may start tomorrow morning then. Nine o'clock sharp, please."

Over the next few weeks Violet took to the job like a natural. Learning how to deal with customers – how to charm them, learning just how far to go with flattery to ensure a sale, to win, as she saw it – became an obsession.

Life at 'Belle Vue Sur La Mer' was ruled over by Aunt Alice, who very much liked and knew the order of things and how they should be done, which she swiftly imposed upon Violet. Under Alice's tutorage Violet acquired some badly-needed polish, soon learning to speak in a better way and groom herself with the utmost care, in short, she acquired a different persona, transforming herself into a snappy young lady about town. Every morning before she went to work she religiously applied three drops of the fashionable '4711 Eau de Cologne' behind each ear and, daringly, behind both knees.

In time it emerged that Aunt Alice was a subversive suffragette and she encouraged Violet to wave the banner for the cause, but in that she was not so successful. Violet certainly admired her independent-minded sisters and totally believed, as Eve did, that women were the equal to men, but unlike Eve, she was no suffragette. In fact in the company of her adored cousins, Bertie and Geoffrey, or any man, come to that, she soon learned to play dumb and keep her mouth shut about politics.

Bertie and Geoffrey were delightful boys, clean-cut, good-looking and funny. Scholars and sportsmen, they'd just left Brighton College. Geoffrey was planning on a military career, like his father, but fair-haired Bertie was more of a good-time boy, uncertain whether to improve his undoubted talents at University or go straight to work in the city. They both were mad about jazz, and were always set on having a 'larky time'. They peppered their conversation with unintelligible words like 'bee's knees', 'cat's meow', 'ducky' and 'swell'.

After three months, Eve came down from London to stay with her aunt, and on Saturday night the two sisters, accompanied by their cousins, Geoffrey and Bertie, went out dancing to the Davis ballroom in Brighton. Violet had her hair bobbed in the latest style and had forgotten all about her singing ambitions, she now fancied herself as a flapper. Eve was amused to observe how popular she'd become with the local boys – Saturday nights at the Davis ballroom were apparently a regular event – how they crowded around her. Violet appeared to be in blue heaven being the centre of attention, like a regular little Scarlett O'Hara. That was the night she first met cousin Bertie's chum, Bernard.

The following morning she crept into Evelyn's bed for a cuddle.

'Oh, Eve,' she cooed, 'I don't know what's come over me. I'm all goofy. That Bernard's the bee's knees and cat's pyjamas all rolled into one. He's the spiffiest handsomest boy I ever met. Lovely wavy hair, so tall, and what a dancer! When he put his hand on my spine, Oh, Lordy! I just shivered. He's a proper gent, too. We did the tango, then a waltz and it was like dancing on air. He didn't talk much, but I could feel his body through my dress and just knew what he was thinking by the way he looked at me. Great blue eyes he's got. Made me feel all gooey. I hardly danced with anyone else all evening. He's got a model T Ford, too, and he drove me home in it. You know the one I mean. Did you like him?"

"He was certainly very handsome," answered Eve. "Though I confess I was somewhat bewildered when he called me a 'hep hotsy-totsy'."

"Oh, Eve, get with it," Vi giggled. "That's a compliment. You carry on like you're some old married lady."

"Well, I am," Eve replied. "I'm thirty-one, and all of you lot are mere teenagers."

"There's nothing 'mere' about me, darling!" said Violet, raising her plucked eyebrows in affectation. "Or that divine man Bernard, he's the real McCoy, as are Geoffrey and Bertie."

Violet adored her cousins. Soon she was accompanying them on all their weekend jaunts. They went to house parties, point-to-points, to the Brighton race track; they sailed on yachts and had beach parties. Eve even had a postcard from her from Le Touquet, which, in those days was the playground for a very racy set. Violet had always been nifty with a needle and now she was running up her own frocks on Mrs Bloom's sewing machine (after hours), for friends as well, selling them, copying them from fashion magazines. At eighteen she was presenting herself like a fashion plate, painted-up with lipstick and mascara on her lashes, smoking, drinking cocktails, and going to the films. She thought of her life then as a film and she very definitely was the star.

A year later, just after Violet's nineteenth birthday, Eve's telephone in London rang.

'I have to see you, Eve,' said Violet. 'Can I pop up to Paddington for the weekend?'

'Of course,' answered Eve. 'Why, what is it? What's so important?'

'I can't tell you on the phone. Must dash, see you Saturday.'

Finally, after she arrived and the sisters were alone, she came out with it. 'I'm pregnant.'

'Oh, Lordy,' said Eve, appalled, but hardly surprised. 'Who's the father?'

'That's the problem. I don't know! I'm thrilled about having a baby, I mean, I am, really, and I'm going to have it, it's just that... I'm not too sure who the father is. There, I've told you.'

Eve's heart sank. In 1929 having a child out of wedlock was considered a major misdemeanour. It meant being consigned to social death, apart from the practical difficulties and misery of trying to raise a child alone. Horrified, she gasped, 'What on earth are you telling me?'

'I've been making whoopee with two of the most beautiful men you've ever seen, and I don't know who the father is. Simple! Is that plain enough for you?'

Eve frowned. 'You mean in an orgy?'

Vi hooted with laughter. 'Good heavens, Eve! I'm not steeped in sin that far. It's just that I have two boyfriends, Bernard and William, that's all. Bernard took me to the opening of *So This Is Love* with Madge Elliot and Cyril Richard at the Winter Garden the other month and we stayed the night at the Strand Palace. The other time was, well, I admit, a bit earthier, on the Downs with William Dancy, but it was a simply heavenly day, and he owns most of it, simply acres!'

She was acting so devil-may-care, but underneath, Eve could see she was really scared stiff. "Darling," she said, "you're in no position to bring up a child alone. Nice girls just don't do that sort of thing."

"Neither do they have abortions," said Vi, chewing her lip. "I'm not having one of those."

Eve felt useless. She knew nothing whatever about that sort of thing. Her sister had come to her in trouble, wanting her help, and she was unable to give it.

'I'm not sure I should be telling you this, Billy,' said Evelyn, suddenly addressing me. I was quite taken aback to be spoken to so directly. I'd become so immersed in her story, it had become like a film playing in my head. Nevertheless I grinned at her encouragingly.

'But, you're a grown man now,' she continued, 'and in some ways I think it answers your question. In my opinion, that was responsible for what happened later. But she wanted you, Billy. Oh yes, she wanted you so much.'

'So what happened?' I asked.

'Well, I gave her the third degree. "So which of these two Romeos do you love, then?"'

Immediately I was back in time again. There sat my vivacious young mother on Eve's sofa in Paddington, her silk-stocked legs crossed, dressed in all her 1920s finery.

"Bernard, of course," she answered gaily. "I'm crazy about him. I only went out with William to make him jealous. Bernard's by far the richest. But then, William is gorgeous too. He's absolutely loaded."

"You can't marry both of them, pull yourself together, girl," said Eve. "All I can say is, you'd better make sure one of them pops the question double quick before you start to show."

"Quite," answered Vi. *I had better do something about that.*

Within a week Eve received another phone call.

"Bernard's proposed!" laughed Vi down the line.

"'Thank heaven for that!'" said Eve, with a sigh. "Congratulations! And guess what?"

"What?"

"Len's firm is being relocated to Kemp Town. It's serendipity. The office is only a mile or two away from you in Hove. So we're having to up sticks and move."

"Oh, Eve. What a palaver!"

"Don't worry. The flat here is only rented, but moving down to Brighton means I can be on hand to help arrange the wedding. Won't that be fun? Mind you, we'll have to act quickly. A certain haste is required in the matter. After all, we can't have you walking down the aisle *enceinte,* can we? Have you told Aunt Alice yet?"

"Certainly not."

"Better do so, and quickly. You can hardly tell her the truth, of course. She'd be horrified and probably disown you. She's bound to be shocked as it is. I mean, that you've got yourself engaged. Let's face it, darling, you will have to shift."

But Aunt Alice's reaction to the news was quite the reverse of Eve's expectation.

"Violet, my darling. How very delightful. I'm so happy for you. Bernard is a perfect choice, such a gentleman. I've often thought what a good example he sets to Bertie, who, I admit, can be a little headstrong. Now, you must allow me to pay for everything. No arguments. Not having a daughter of my own, I shall enjoy myself enormously. Indulge me, do. Your dear mother, bless her, will hardly be able to afford to pay for the kind of reception that will be required. It will have to be at 'The Grand', of course. I shall ask her to come and stay here with the twins – who will both have to be fitted out as bridesmaids......" and on she went, greatly excited by the news and the arrangements she was going to have to make.

The wedding day eventually arrived. Everyone appeared in their best, Violet looked ravishing in white lace, naturally. Neither Alice nor Muzz had a notion of what had really gone on, however, a certain group of wedding guests, the Brighton set, suspected. Still, nothing was actually said, there was no incriminating bulge to mar the general rejoicing and everything appeared respectable.

Bernard bought an attractive little house in Ventnor Villas in Hove, just a few streets away from Aunt Alice. Violet stopped work but still had an itch. She was not content. "Being a housewife is really boring," she confided to Linda, who by this time had become her best friend. She was still yearning for the stars and the limelight.

"I'm a born milliner!" she announced to Bernard one evening across their brand new mahogany dining table. "I'm much better at making hats than that Mrs Bloom. Linda tells me she wants to retire. Could you afford to buy me her hat shop?"

So Bernard made her an offer.

Mrs Bloom accepted and the millinery business transferred into Violet's name. Linda's father, a charming gentleman called Mr Thompson, offered to chip in with a few thousand, and Linda became Vi's partner. Thus 'Philinda's' was born. Meanwhile a less than flattering bump was spoiling the fall of Violet's sexy loose flapper dresses.

"Billy Boy's arrival really set the cat amongst the pigeons," said Eve, again switching me sharply back into her chintzy sitting room in Folkstone. "I have to tell you, Billy, your Mum went potty, and not just mildly so. Right round the bend, she went. I was there, I saw it happen. She had that condition, what's it called now? A lot of women had it in those days, highly-strung women like your mother, after giving birth. Postpartum necrosis, that's it. She's unloving towards you, suffers guilt for having such feelings, and she can't sleep. She loves children, she says, but only wants a little girl she can dress up and pet. Now she has you, a boy, she rejects you. Bernard is out at his office all day, because, of course, he's the boss and has to be there. Vi's not seen her other boyfriend, William Dancy for months, so what does the silly bitch go and do? Can you believe, she goes for a walk along the promenade and meets him? Whether by accident or intent, I never found out, but they meet. You're lying in your pram staring up with your baby blues.

'Sure he isn't mine?' says William looking into the pram. 'He looks as if he might be.'

Well, she frets herself into a fine old how-do-you-do. She convinces herself she's married the wrong man, the wrong father. Over the weeks she winds herself up into such a state she has a nervous breakdown and has to be carted off to a nursing home. You're barely seven months old and shoved out of the way to some nanny or other, Joe's first wife, I think it was. Linda, meanwhile, is having to look after 'Philinda's' alone, and incidentally, cook supper for your Dad in the evenings when he comes back from work.

Three months later Violet returns to Ventnor Villas and you're brought home, but she's still unstable. Well, she always was a hot-headed girl. She must have been pretty hellish to live with for your poor father. Though I don't think that's what drove him away, I think it was that business with William Dancy. Mind you, he did rather fall for your mother's friend, Linda, who, I admit, was a very sweet girl. When the two of them walked out on her, that was it, Vi really did go bananas. Completely haywire, she went. Those were her darkest days. 'He's my whole life,' she howls. 'I can't live without him. He can't leave me.' She practically screams the house down. 'He loves me. I know he loves me really, not her. She's my best friend!' She's inconsolable, sobbing and carrying on something chronic. 'Everything I know about life, everything I understand, I understand because I love him,' she says, misquoting Leo Tolstoy – not that she realised that, of course. She becomes obsessed with getting him back – and, as you know, years later she succeeded – she goes out onto the streets searching for him, goes AWOL. Has a complete mental collapse. She walked out of the hat shop leaving you, an eighteen-month-old baby, all alone in that workroom for three whole days before it occurs to us that she might have taken off without you. Anything could have happened. Abandoned, you were. You could have starved, died, anything. She was wandering all over Brighton and God knows where, looking for him. The police eventually found her on the beach by the ship yards near Saltdean.

I was the one who found you, Billy. Crawling on all fours, you were. You'd not had any food or water for days, but apart from the mess you were in, you were amazingly cheerful. The shop front was locked-up, so we had to break in through the back way, and the first thing you did was hold a pin up to me that you'd found on the floor. 'Min, min, min', you said. I think they were the first words you ever spoke.

Aunt Alice's doctor recommended a private mental hospital, and she was taken there. They strapped her down, applied electrodes to her temples and gave her electric shock treatment. Burns, here, on either side of her head, she had afterwards. Simply dreadful!

This time you were packed off to a proper foster home and then to that Institution on the Isle of Wight. St Catherine's, I think it was called. You were there for nearly six years.

Your mother wasn't in the mental home that long, but by the time she'd sorted herself out, which was about eighteen months later, she didn't want you.

She was in no fit state to look after you, Billy. When she came out, she was a different woman. She'd lost all that wonderful vivacity. All her vitality had just drained away, all her go, just vanished. She spent most of her days at the picture house seeing films; she didn't seem able to connect with real life. Escaping, she was. I used to go over to the house to check on her whenever I could. Gradually she improved, of course, but thereafter I remember everything had to be as neat and as tidy as a new pin, as perfect as it was in *Good Housekeeping*. The cutlery in her kitchen had to be put away perfectly, all the knives, forks and spoons in the drawer neatly arranged on top of each other.

Linda, can you believe, was back running 'Philinda's' by this time. Well, it was her shop too, she was a partner. There was some story of your father deserting her for a nurse. But he was not a healthy man. He'd contracted tuberculosis and was in a sanatorium. Your mother and Linda made it up and became friends again, but it was an uncomfortable time, because the lawyers were then dealing with the divorce. Bernard made her a very generous settlement, though, I must say. He gave her both the house and the shop. The marriage had lasted barely three-and-a-half years.

It wasn't until four years later, after your mother had got herself hitched up with Stan and they rented that bungalow in Selsey Bill, that she felt strong enough to bring you back. Before then, while she was on the hunt for a new man, you'd have got in her way, cramped her style.

I couldn't have looked after you, Billy, not at that time. Len and I discussed it, but we were in the throes of running our new business in Kemp Town. But you turned out all right in the end, didn't you, love? Despite being shoved out of everyone's way all the time. Boarding schools all the way. Oh, my goodness, just look at the time. How I've been rattling on. You'll be wanting to get home to your Annie."

133

Chapter Twenty

Pop-Goes-Your-Heart

1976/7

Driving home from Evelyn's apartment that evening I chewed over everything she'd told me. So many things were clearer, so many questions answered. The least of which was, why I remembered that workroom at 'Philinda's' so vividly.

Now I understood why I'd been dumped in foster homes and in that Institution on the Isle of Wight, and why William Dancy had taken me out for Sunday lunch years ago at school. The poor guy had been checking me out to see if I was his son. But the young girl Evelyn had described seemed a far cry from the predatory Joan Crawford-type mother I knew. Did I understand her any the better? A little, but mainly the story had left me with an unaccustomed sympathy for her.

Three months later 'Pop-Goes-Your-Heart', my Uncle Ralph's seventy-something-year-old widow came over from Worthing to see the matinée of the play I was appearing in at the Theatre Royal, Brighton, for, as I'd promised myself, I'd managed to extricate myself from the television soap and was now touring the provinces in a new farce destined for the West End. After the performance we had tea in a café in Bond Street near the theatre. I was thrilled to see her. Her bugle beads still hung down over her flat chest, but I was saddened to see how thin and fragile she'd become. Her hair was now quite white.

"You always used to make me laugh when you were a wee lad," she said, her cheeks flushed with excitement. "And you certainly did this afternoon. You play that 'silly ass' part to perfection."

"Thank you, darling," I said, "I'll take that as a compliment. Now tell me, how are things? I mean you. How are you, really?"

"Well," she said, suddenly flustered and polishing her teaspoon with a napkin. "I'm fine. I admit it's very difficult without Ralph. I miss him terribly..." she stopped and firmly put down the spoon. "Oh dear, I'm so sorry." I thought for a moment she was going to cry, but she looked up and attempted a smile. "I'm trying to pretend everything's all right, and it isn't. It isn't at all. Oh, Billy, I never thought I'd say this, but I do get so terribly lonely without him. You see, I've always been such a busy person all my life. I have to tell you something. I've come to a decision. I'm going to sell the bungalow and move in with a friend."

"Which friend is that, darling?" I asked. "Do I know them?"

"She's a new friend," she answered. "I only met her the other month. I was sitting on a bench on the promenade gazing out to sea thinking how life changes us all and how strong we have to be, when someone asked, 'Would you like a chocolate?' I must have been in a brown study for I looked up and this young woman was on my bench. I'd never even noticed her sit down. She looked a nice enough type, but no, I thought, never take sweets from a stranger, wasn't that silly? Still, I thought, it would be nice to talk to someone, so I said, 'How kind of you,' and I accepted one. The two of us started chatting, and she told me all about herself. How her husband had deserted her and how lonely she was, left alone, like me, rattling about in one of those houses overlooking the seafront at Ferring. I told her of my situation, and how I felt exactly the same in my little bungalow. She's such a nice young woman," Auntie eagerly explained to me. "We've met up several times since for coffee mornings. Well, the other day she suggested

135

I sell my bungalow and go and live with her. We'd be companions for each other, you see, and she's offered to look after me, too."

Yes, I thought, then shove you down the stairs and take your savings. "Darling," I said, "do you think that's quite wise? I mean if you've only just met the woman?"

"Oh, she a very nice class of person, and she tells me she has training in looking after old people. We've become very close these last few weeks."

As tactfully as I could I explained that this action might not be in her best interest, that perhaps it would be wiser to find a congenial Care Home. But Pop-Goes-Your-Heart was adamant; loneliness had decided her and that was that, she'd take no advice from me. I was still 'little Billy boy' who'd turned up naked and shivering on her front doorstep all those years ago in Ayr; I may have grown up, but I was no wiser now that the silly-ass cuckold husband I was portraying in the farce she'd just seen, how could I possibly understand her feelings of desolation and know what was best?

The one person I knew she would listen to was Mother. Pop-Goes-Your-Heart may not care much for her ex-sister-in-law, but Violet had once run a hat shop, been a business woman, they were of an age and had known each other a lifetime.

I wrote to Mother explaining that I thought Pop-Goes-Your-Heart was about to become the victim of a confidence trickster. ".....So if you could possibly say something to her, explain that she'd have better care and treatment in a proper Care Home. I'm sure she'd listen to you, Mother. I would so hate to see her swindled out of her life savings by some con woman.

I should be most grateful for your help. Love Billy. XX"

Mother wrote back agreeing to meet me in Folkestone, where she'd recently moved to be nearer her sister, Evelyn. She said she'd sold the Barham cottage, "very well indeed" and bought a mansion flat. However, we were not to meet there; she suggested we rendezvous for lunch at the Clifton Hotel, a grand hotel on The Leas, a no-man's land and neutral territory. We arranged it for a Sunday, my day off from touring the farce. Annie was away still filming her six-part television series on the Isle of Man – we spoke on the telephone nearly every day and she was enjoying herself hugely being treated like a star – the children were being looked after by their other grandmother, so I travelled to Folkestone by train. Nearly seven months had lapsed since that evening in Joe's house when she'd told me she never wanted to see me again.

I made my way to the Leas, and Regency-style Clifton Hotel. There, in an almost deserted bar overlooking the sun terrace, I found her waiting for me, sitting on a sofa upholstered in faded floral, holding a large a gin and tonic. She was wearing a pale camel-haired coat with a brightly-coloured Jacmar scarf draped over her shoulders; it was hard to believe she'd been as ill as Evelyn had reported to me, for as usual she looked terrific.

She eyed me warily. "I know perfectly well why you're asking me to do this," she said, coming straight to the point and clutching her crocodile-skin handbag to her side. "You want me to ensure that you inherit Stella's estate for you, don't you?" Mother would never deign to call her, 'Pop-Goes-Your-Heart'.

"Well, yes," I admitted, "that thought had occurred to me."

"Just as well," she replied, "'cause you'll get nothing from me when I trade in my clogs."

The unlikely notion of Mother trading in clogs did not blind me to the slap in the face she was delivering.

"With all the hardships I've had to endure," she continued, "you've not exactly been a dutiful son, have you?" She glared at me.

I was speechless.

"I'll do it, mind," she continued, "because I think you deserve to get something from your father's side of the family. They never came up with a penny to help with your education after he left me. I've never thought your Aunt Stella was the sharpest knife in the box, so I can't say I'm surprised she's fallen foul for some flim-flam con artist. Personally I thought she was a wet sack, but nevertheless I've telephoned her and she's invited me over next Friday. If I go, and I repeat if, I'd be doing it for you, my boy, for you. Now then, tell me about my grandchildren, have you got any photos for me. How's Annie? I saw her on television the other evening looking lovely. It's such a pity you left that telly series you were in, we never see anything of you these days. Are you working at all?"

So there it was; she would do as I requested if I would play the part of the dutiful son.

I did, and we staggered through lunch.

Mother did go to see Pop-Goes-Your-Heart in Worthing the following Friday, and even drove her around to audition Nursing Homes. Auntie sold her bungalow and after taking Mother's advice moved into the Care Home they'd chosen. I visited her there several times. It was an old country house where she was permitted to move in some of her own furniture. Sadly, she soon lost the will to live and, after only six months, died.

"How tragic," said Mother on the telephone when I told her. "I've known Stella half my life. As you know I never go to funerals, but in her case, I suppose I really should make an effort. I first met her with your father over forty years ago. I expect I'll be her oldest friend there."

Annie was on tour at the time, starring in a revival of a Somerset Maugham play and couldn't come to the funeral, so I went alone. I met Mother in the car park of the Worthing crematorium, the very same crematorium where she'd refused to speak to me at

Ralph's funeral three years ago. She arrived in a chauffeur-driven car. As we milled about waiting for the previous funeral to finish, on the conveyor belt of death, she was suspiciously quiet. I had the uneasy feeling she had an agenda and was cooking something up beneath her best black hat, for there was more than just reverential respect in her silence.

No sooner had the chapel doors opened than she made a bee line for the front pew. I knew then we were done for. Sombre formality and pew entitlement seemed to give Mother carte blanche to let rip. I waited on tenterhooks. As the service was ending and I was beginning to think we might just have got away with it, just as we were standing for Pop-Goes-Your-Heart's coffin to slide out of sight into the furnace, Mother started. She burst into song. "Roses round the door/ Babies on the floor/ that's what I adore/ Sleepy valley." She sang the popular thirties song as if it were a hymn, con brio, and she definitely hooked her audience.

The curtain around the coffin slowly closed. "Mother!" I hissed. "Be quiet."

"She so loved that song," she sobbed, sinking to her knees in the appearance of prayer. "Your father used to sing it to her. He teased her unmercifully. Oh, that man! Dear God! Stella never had any babies, you see. Babies on the floor... babies! He used to die." Out came the tears, the prop handkerchief. "Darling Stella...Bernard...babies... you were my last baby," she gasped. "I could never have any more children after you. You ripped the womb out of me."

Oh, Lord! I thought. Not that again. Here we go. She was on a roll, under the guise of grief she was punishing me for the years of silence. Like the scheming serpent she was, she was getting her own back for me not driving her home to Barham, plus, of course, enjoying an emotion wallow. "Mother," I seethed, "Stop it."

"I couldn't have any more babies after you. We tried, but it was a stillborn. Had it lived it would have been your half-sister. Like a dead doll, it was."

Even the hymn musak failed to cover Mother's self-pitying faux grief.

The mourners behind were riveted, nobody moved.

"Mother, come along now," I hissed. For the benefit of the vicar and congregation I went through the motions of comforting her, but my jaw was clenched and my hands were steel as I tried to prize her out of the pew. But she was only just getting into her stride. A bulldozer couldn't have stopped her now.

"A little sister you would have had." With a martyred expression she clasped her arms round her stomach and rocked herself to and fro. On and on she went. "You never knew that did you? I tried to keep it from you, wanted to protect you. I never wanted you to know what I suffered. But oh yes, I always wanted another child. So did Stanley, poor man, a child of his own. You never cared for him, did you? And he knew it, oh yes. And he made so many sacrifices for you. Worked his fingers to the bone to educate you, send you to that school....a fat lot you cared."

The congregation, damn them, were spellbound. She turned herself in profile to them so they all had a better view.

"My frail body couldn't give him a child. You saw to that. Dead, it was, just like dear Stella over there. Dear, darling Stella." Whimpers punctuated her every utterance. "And when I was in hospital, when I nearly died, you never came near me. You never spoke to me in all those years. Ten years of silence...not a word. What sort of a son behaves like that to his mother?"

"We have to leave now, Mother."

The vicar was approaching with a glass of water, his face contorted into a semblance of sympathy.

"What have I ever done to you that you never came near me in all those years? I nearly died, I did."

I'd had enough. So apparently had the congregation, thankfully they were beginning to file out.

"But you didn't die, did you, Mother? And I'm here now. So buck up!" I gripped her arm and forced her to stand to accept the glass from the vicar.

"Thank you so much, Vicar. Do forgive my distress, Stella and I shared so much in life. "

"I quite understand," he answered.

With my eyebrow cynically raised I watched her drink. After one sip I snatched the glass away and returned it to the vicar. "Thank you so much," I said, and sternly led her out.

The exit passage led to a display of flowers and wreaths laid out in a courtyard. I stopped to read the messages. Mother ignored them and walked on.

I was furious with her, yet philosophical. Had I really expected her to behave properly at such a time? Of course not. But how dare she use Pop-Goes-Your-Heart's funeral for this attack on me, which, of course had found its mark. I'd wanted the ground to open up and swallow me. We said goodbye curtly and she sat in the back of her chauffeur-driven car looking very pleased with herself, smug like a burst boil. She'd got it all out.

A month later I had a letter from Auntie Pop-Goes-Your-Heart's solicitor informing me that I was her sole beneficiary, but by then events had changed so much I hardly cared. My life had suddenly collapsed and spiralled into a pit of despair. I was shattered, or as a tabloid newspaper at the time put it, "Old Roly falls apart". This was in reference to my soap-opera persona; under the headline was a photograph of me tripping up in the street as I was leaving 'Stringfellows' nightclub looking drunk, next to it was another photograph, one of my glamorous wife, Annie Bartlett, arm in arm with her new lover.

Chapter Twenty-One

An Egg Whisk

1977/8

"I knew it," said Mother when I told her on the telephone that Annie had left me. "I knew she was a bitch the moment I set eyes on her."

Even as my heart was bleeding and the pain of red-hot coals burning in my breast tormented me, I laughed. The years of aggravation between us melted for a moment and I loved her for being so unequivocally on my side. Nevertheless I couldn't stop myself pointing out that, "When you first met her you said she was so beautiful you could eat her up!"

"Well, you were so bewitched, I had to say something." Then lowering her voice to her wisdom-wise tones, she added, "She drove a wedge between us, Billy, you know that, don't you?" Then, as practical as ever, "Anyway where's she gone and what about the children?"

"She says she's fallen in love with some actor she's been working with. She's moved in to his love nest in Hampstead. Actually, he was my understudy in a play I did years ago. Some would say he still is!"

"Oh, my dear Billy, I know exactly what you're going through, your father did exactly the same thing to me when you were a baby. But tell me, dear, did you not suspect something was going on?"

"She's been on location for the last three months, I've hardly seen her. When we did see each other at the odd weekend she seemed okay. Now I come to think about it, though, she did seem a bit funny, sort of distant, but I put that down to her being absorbed in her work. I get a bit blinkered myself when I'm working."

"What about the children?"

"They're at school. I'm at the Savoy Theatre doing eight shows a week in this farce and going crazy trying to cope. Matinée days are murder. I've got a mother's help in, but I'm worried Annie might turn up while I'm at work and snatch the children, or even take the furniture. Do you think you could possibly come and look after them for me, Mother? You're the only person I can trust."

"My dear, of course. It will be an opportunity for me to get to know my grandchildren better. Of course I'll come."

And to my surprise she did. For the first time in twenty years she made the journey up to London. It was a cold harsh November and Mother slept on the sofa bed in my study. But, alas, she was not oil on troubled waters. Violet, the eternal drama queen, was more like an egg whisk.

Returning home from the theatre one night, my thirteen-year-old daughter Rebecca was waiting up for me. Tearfully she related, "Mummy rang us up while you were at work. Grandma answered the phone in the kitchen while we were having supper. She called Mumma a bitch for deserting us; she called her other beastly names, too, right in front of us. I think Grandma's horrid. I want her to leave, I hate her."

The next day their headmistress – whom I'd already informed of our situation – telephoned to say that Annie had attempted to kidnap James from school, Mother took the call as I was out of the house. I arrived back to find James had been sent home in a taxi. Rebecca was out on a school trip. Within quarter of an hour the front-door bell rang. I answered it.

There on the door step stood my beloved but faithless wife. I'd not seen her for two months and my emotions escalated to a fever pitch. She was wearing unfamiliar clothes and on her face was an expression I'd never seen before. Alas, it was not that of the penitent wife returning to the bosom of her family, on the contrary her proud demeanour and high colour denoted a very different agenda. I felt as if I was standing next to a volcano.

"I've come for the children." Her role was now that of the noble mother wronged.

I bared the way with my body.

Behind me at the top of the stairs stood my mother clutching James.

"Violet," cried Annie. "You're a mother, let me have my child."

Violet paused, then released my son, who ran down the stairs into his mother's arms.

I couldn't fight all three of them. I felt as if my life was ebbing away. There was a light dusting of snow on the ground outside and I turned to the coat rack at the end of the hall to fetch James's duffle coat. When I returned to the front door, they'd both vanished.

I ran into the street after them to fasten James's coat around him. That was the last I saw of my darling son for six months. Later, I had a letter from him, probably dictated by his mother, it said: *"I love you very much but want to live with Mumma."*

By the time Rebecca returned home from her school outing, I had had to leave for the theatre. Discovering that her baby brother had left home, she was distraught. Grandma was not a good substitute. In the middle of the night she ran away to join her mother and brother in the dreaded Hampstead love nest.

It wasn't until breakfast that I discovered I'd been well and truly dumped.

Mother took her fury out on the refrigerator. I'll never forget her on her hands and knees stabbing the ice box with a carving knife intent on chipping away the ice, under her breath cursing Annie. After lunch she went back home to Folkestone and I was left with the cat...the children's cat that I'd taken in as a kitten for them both. And being a dog sort of person, I can do without cats. Alone, I wandered round my deserted home, the pain of red-hot coals burning in my breast flared up into a furnace.

With three months left on my contract at the theatre, I had to somehow hold it together and go on every night. The farce was a huge success, a sell out; but like 'Pagliacci', every time I opened my mouth some 2000 audience members roared with laughter, yet inside I was breaking apart, an emotional wreck. I was walking-wounded and weeping with misery. However, acting is a strange business, Doctor Theatre takes care of you; when I look back on that unhappy period, I realise it was the play that saved me and kept me sane, without it I might have topped myself.

Friends helped me, too. When you're going through a divorce you get to know who your true friends really are. In my case I lost half our phone book. Among the people who were constant and never wavered, was Violet.

When my contract expired, the management re-cast the play and it continued without me. I spent Christmas with my film director friend from Carlisle rep days and his family.

"C'mon," he said, trying to talk some sense into me. "Can't you see what a favour she's done you? Now you're free to be your true self."

At the time I couldn't see what he meant and was furious. "But I always have been my true self," I answered.

"Believe me, you're well out of it," he counselled, "She'd become a chromium-plated diva. You couldn't see it, but I could. Who needs a wife like that?"

I did. I missed her so terribly.

For New Year I went to stay with Mother in her newly-decorated but not yet fully appointed mansion flat in Folkestone. It was the closest time we ever had together and one evening I asked her about Father. I didn't quite have the pluck to admit, "I was under the bed when you suffocated him," though I was tempted, but I did ask:

"Is it true what Uncle Ralph told me, that you turned up in 1939 at The Branksome Towers Hotel, Bournemouth at my father's second wedding?"

"I certainly did," she answered. "I wasn't going to let him marry that bitch!"

"And did you and Stan really take him back to live with you?"

"I did. Well, it was me your father really loved."

"So you lived with your two husbands in a ménage a trois?"

"I did."

"Which one did you sleep with, Mother?"

Shock horror appeared on her face. "The one I was married to, of course."

"And what happened to Winifred, the girl he was going marry?"

"Ah well, when your father died, Stan said we ought to tell her. I wasn't going to, but he, the bloody fool, wrote and told her so. And what do you think she did?"

Knowing by her tone that something good was coming, I gave her the cue. "I've no idea Mother, what?"

"She sent me the bill for the filthy night the two of them had spent at The Branksome Towers Hotel six months beforehand!"

With my divorce case pending, I was offered an excellent part – not as Violet would say 'a nice part' for it was to portray a decadent Turkish officer – in an all male production of a Terence Rattigan play that was going to Canada. It was a perfect opportunity, a chance to leave the geography of my misery. Devastating as losing my children was to me, how could I foresee it was to prove my salvation? My 'freedom pass' to wherever the winds of Fate would blow me. It seemed they were blowing me to Canada.

So I put the house up for sale with an estate agent and flew to Toronto. There, without wife, children or mother, my life would take on a new direction and, at the age of forty-eight, alter my existence utterly.

Chapter Twenty-Two

At L'hotel

1978

Toronto was covered in a great white eiderdown of snow. Driving to the city centre from the airport all was crisp, cold and exciting. I huddled in the Mercedes People Carrier grateful for my new British Warm sheepskin overcoat. In the far distance the tops of skyscrapers vanished into wisps of cloud. 'L'Hotel', the chic hotel I'd been allocated, was in Downtown Toronto and stood next to the C.N. Tower, the world's tallest building, and only a short walk from the Alexander Theatre where we were to appear. The Canadians seemed mostly to be wearing puffer jackets, jeans and sunglasses, the women, fur and elegant boots. The contrast inside the hotel was amazing. In the vast Reception area there was suddenly warmth; marble floors, glass and chrome, palm trees, rich carpets and even a small waterfall. The other guests, divesting themselves of their protective coats, appeared in T-shirts and light clothing. Everyone to my eyes looked bright, sexy and attractive.

The play was a hit, a huge hit. We were bombarded with invitations. There were charity lunches to attend, late-night movie premiers, Galas, parties, matinées of other productions, even offers from wealthy patrons to spend Sundays in their homes. No one (except the cast, who were all, to a man, terrific chaps) knew anything of my private life and I was judged purely on what people made of me on stage. My hair was cropped into a military style for the production and I grew a beard. It grew out black and white and, in one scene, I appeared in nothing more than a scarlet waist-coat with an eastern nappy-style outfit of the type Yul Brunner wore in 'The King and I'; with my tanned body make-up I thought I looked the bee's knees. Actors are finely tuned to compliments and I soon realised that others had similar thoughts for I found myself courted by both ladies and gentlemen. Sometimes their approach was subtle; sometimes they were downright flirtatious and frank. I took no offence; to be admired and desired did wonders for my shipwrecked self-esteem. I was now heart-free, after all, the bonds of marriage and fidelity had withered and died. I was in a situation to take full advantage of the hospitality on offer, and I knew moments of joy that reminded me of that other guy, the young guy I used to be, the one I'd forced myself to forget throughout my married years. Sex helped blot out the pain, the helplessness I felt at the three people I loved most in the world being with another man. The hurt in my heart eased and I became aware of new elation within me, an excitement, a confidence and strength unknown. It passed swiftly, as all such moments do, but I realised that something that had lain dormant within me was now unleashed. Was this the real self my old friend had talked about?

One afternoon after accepting a delicious lunch from a hospitable widow, she suggested coffee in her living room. I sat on the sofa and she leant over to kiss me. Moments later we were entangled in each other's arms. Her twenty-something-year-old son suddenly walked into the room. My lady friend was most put-out, but I only thought how much more desirable the son was than the mother.

Another time I was in bed with a beautiful nineteen-year-old girl, not much older than my daughter. As we were cuddling she started to sob. "Whatever is the matter," I asked.

"I'm so sorry," she cried. "I can't go through with this. I'm a lesbian!"

"Funny you should say that," I answered. "'Cause I think I'm gay too."

We grinned at each other and spent the rest of the weekend taking long walks around the lake exchanging experiences and talking about our emotions. We are still in touch and she became a great friend.

I also became friends with the director of the electricity company and his wife. They were Hungarians and told me they'd fled the revolution in 1956. They'd been students at the time and had escaped on bicycles with their books and belongings. As they approached the Austrian border they'd had to drop everything and run. They'd come to Canada as refugees, not knowing the language, and had somehow managed to make this great success of their lives. They were a charming couple and invited me to their lakeside house outside Toronto. I asked why was it that the lights in the city skyscrapers stayed on all night. Wasn't that a dreadful waste of electricity? He explained that if the lights were switched off in the evening, the demand the next day when everyone turned them again would be so immense it would overload the system and crash.

The management hired me a hairdresser who attended me at 'L'Hotel'. He was an attractive young fellow and gay. He took it upon himself to show me around town and introduce me to his friends; I was taken to gay clubs, bars and saunas, where the guys I met wanted exactly what I wanted; uncomplicated sex with no strings. AIDs was then on the scene, so I took extra care to be safe.

Breakfast in 'L' Hotel' was not served at separate tables like it is in English hotels but at a long table in a large airy dining hall. Each morning when I came down I noticed a handsome Arab gentleman eating alone. He wore a ghutra headdress and aba robe, and after a day or two we exchanged nods, but there was, I sensed, an interest between us beyond mere courtesy. One morning we sat opposite each other and he introduced himself. His handshake was warm and strong. He told me he was a prince and had been to see me in my play the previous evening. He said he had enjoyed it and had a proposition to put to me. Over breakfast, with the theatre programme before him with my C.V. in it, he explained he was starting up a new television station in his country and needed someone to run the Drama department, would I be interested? The contract he suggested would be for five years and the salary, when he mentioned a prospective figure, was eye watering. His sexy smile and hooded black eyes promised 'strings attached', and for a brief moment I saw myself as a rich man's plaything, but the phrase 'put not your trust in princes' came to mind. Anyway I was unavailable, for I'd signed a contract to open the play later in the year at the 'Old Vic' in London. I considered his offer for all of thirty seconds before declining. I could never have changed my life so radically, but it did prove to me such things were possible. What was I thinking of? I'd already changed my life radically, I realised. I was now gay again, and what's more, I was very happy about it.

Towards the end of my stay in Canada I had a telephone call from Mother.

"Are you sitting down?" she enquired.

"Yes," I answered. "Why, what is it?"

'I'm getting married again."

Oh no, I thought. What poor blighter has she found now?

Chapter Twenty-Three

Majesty of the Seas

1978

Considering the fate of her first three husbands, I was somewhat concerned for the welfare of this new brave gentleman. Interested in the size of his fortune too, for that, possibly, would have a bearing on his fate. I suppose I should have stopped being shocked by Mother's antics years ago, but I admit to being stunned by the news; it's really not what one expects from one's sixty-eight-year-old mother. All I could think of was: So she's finally made it, four husbands, like her heroines Bette Davis and Joan Crawford. What I actually said was: "Congratulations, Mother. I'm happy for you. What's he like? Do you love him?"

"Don't be ridiculous," she snapped back, "I'm not a schoolgirl, but he is rather a darling. I'll send you a snap. His name is Richard Malleson, he's a few years older than me and quite well off, I'm happy to say. Well, at my time of life you have to think of these things. He'll look after me well, and I won't have to worry about going to an old folk's home like your poor Aunt Stella. So you'll be off the hook if I go doolally." (I think she meant get Alzheimer's) "There'll be enough cash around to have help in and be properly looked after in our own home."

"And where will that be?" I asked. "Will you go and live with him, or will he come and live in your flat in Folkestone?"

"I'm not moving into his ghastly place. Great cold stone house it is, like a morgue, ugly great Victorian furniture. No, no, he'll have to fit in with me. And he should be so lucky; it's a lovely flat, as you know. There are no stairs to worry about because it's on the ground floor, and the spare room has an en-suite bathroom. It'll suit us just tickety-boo. He is a great dear."

Mmm, I thought, separate bedrooms.

It was a month later she regaled me with how she and Mr Malleson had met. We were sitting on deck-chairs overlooking the Atlantic, a bottle of champagne on the table between us.

"Well," she said, gleefully quaffing back her bubbly, "I was out shopping in Folkestone one morning and it came on to rain. I'd forgotten my umbrella so I popped into 'Fullers'. I sat myself down at a table and ordered a pot of tea. After a while this distinguished gentleman came up and asked if I minded if he shared my table as it was so crowded. I said, "Of course not." and he sat down. Well, he was charming. He had darkish hair but with silver wings, you know. Big boned and authoritative, wearing an attractive Harris Tweed sports jacket. We introduced ourselves and he said used to work in insurance, like your father."

And like you, I thought, but as she was relating this in her grand Queen-of-Sheba manner, wearing a glitter stole over an expensive evening gown and we were in majestic surroundings, I knew she'd not appreciate being reminded of trudging through Clapham council estates collecting bobs and tanners for the Liverpool and Victoria Insurance Company. Not that she was ashamed of her humble heritage, on the contrary, she was perversely proud. "I'm only an Aylesbury duck," she would say, but with such an air of the swan princess about her it was impossible to believe.

"Then it came out that he was a widower," she continued. "So of course I told him I was a widow. Now I look back on it, it was really rather romantic, like Celia Johnson and Trevor Howard in

Brief Encounter, you know. Anyway after tea we said our good-byes and that was that. But I did think what a delightful gentleman he was, cultured too. You'd have liked him, Billy. Anyway it so happened that the very next day, Evelyn and I were out walking on the Leas, and what do you think? There he was sitting on one of the benches looking out to sea. We stopped and had a chat and I introduced him to Eve, and then what? It turned out they knew each other. They'd met years ago when Eve was working in the City and he was a Managing Director of some big company. Of course he was married in those days and lived in Guildford. So we asked him if he'd like to make up a fourth at bridge with us the following week. I'm not mad about bridge myself, I much prefer canasta, as you know, but Eve's an excellent player and it seemed like a good opportunity for a get-together. So he joined us; Eve, her friend Ian Fairbrother, and me. We had a lovely evening, we laughed and joked, and one thing led to another and he asked me out to the pictures the following week, and well, three months later he asked me to marry him." She held her chin up triumphantly. "Fortunately he's comfortably-off, and he is awfully jolly, so I said 'yes' and here we are."

Where we were at the time of this conversation was just off the Bahamas in the middle of the North Atlantic. We were on deck sitting outside the Viking lounge of the Royal Caribbean's Majesty of the Seas cruise-liner on our way to Jamaica. Just how we came to be there, sipping our champers on a warm night with stars twinkling in a clear midnight-blue sky, moonlight glistening on the ocean before us, I will now explain.

Despite Mother's apparent sophistication, she'd never been out of England in her life. She was worldly yet provincial, but with such an impeccable dress-sense she could well have been a model. I don't think she'd ever read a non-fiction book in her life, but I did once spot a Daphne Du Maurier novel in her living room. As far as I know she'd never attended a concert, but she adored music; dance music, Henry Hall and Carol Gibbons, the Warsaw Concerto, Irving Berlin and 'Hutch'. She was racy, yet a prude. Her knowledge of life seemed to be based entirely on movies and her love affairs; which is to say she was a romantic with a nose for money. So when the retired Managing Director, Mr Richard Malleson, asked her one evening when they were planning their wedding: "Where would you like to go for our honeymoon?" She answered,

"My dream would be to go on a Caribbean cruise."

"Then that, my darling Violet," he answered, "is where I shall take you."

In the snap she'd sent me he looked much as she'd described him on the telephone, except to my eyes he also looked somewhat doddery. Though he was grinning in the photo he was also bent double and frankly looked as if he could keel over at any moment. I was not wrong, for on their honeymoon night, that, apparently, is exactly what he did, right on top of Mother, or so she told me. The cable said:

Richard died on first night of cruise. Are you free to take his ticket and continue ten day cruise with me? If so join Majesty of the Seas at midday, Nassau, May 7th. Love Mother.

Immediately I knew my fears had been justified. She'd done it yet again! But how? Had she shoved him overboard? I reckoned she'd fancied a full burial-at-sea type funeral. Visions of her in widow's weeds came to mind, swathed in black, leaning on the Captain's arm as the body of husband number four, draped in the Union Jack, slid into the sea. The band would probably be playing 'You'll Never Walk Alone'.

I was staying with friends in Palm Springs when I received her cable. After the play had closed in Toronto I had a month to fill before it opened in London. Already I'd visited Boston to see relatives and been to Disneyland in Florida, where I'd been miserable, unable to enjoy it alone because my darling children, Rebecca and James, weren't with me. So the prospect of cruising around the Caribbean with Mother for the next ten days did not displease me, besides I was intrigued. I hopped on a plane, changed at Los Angeles, flew to Miami, and thence to Nassau, where I boarded the Majesty of the Seas.

I expected to find her in full mourning. Wrong. She was wearing an attractive deck quoits outfit, cream slacks, silk shirt and sunglasses; and was receiving a great deal of attention from the crew and passengers. I soon realised that in her mind she was Bette Davis in *Now Voyager*, and in fairness to her, she did appear to be the toast of the ship.

"The poor man weighed a ton," she said, telling me about the night Richard had expired on top of her. "I was literally pinned to the bed. I didn't realise what had happened at first. Then, when I tried to move, of course the penny dropped. Well, he was considerably heavier than a penny. But what a wonderful way to go! For him, I mean, certainly it wasn't for me. I mean to say, it was extremely distressing, frightful. I managed to push him off and reach the light switch. When I looked at his face I could tell at once. Out of it, he was, right out of it. Expired with the effort of making love to me, he had. I dressed quickly and called the ship's doctor. Thankfully the man was a gentleman, most understanding. He said he'd known something of the sort happen before with a man of senior years. Huh! Just as I was thinking, everything happens to me! No one's ever going to believe me when I explain how it happened, if I can ever bring myself to tell, that is. Anyway, he examined Richard and confirmed he'd died of a heart attack. Then these dear young sailors came with a stretcher and took him away.

Then the Captain came to see me. Well, he was charm itself. Captain Nondas is his name; he's a smallish man, Greek, and has a little beard, you'll meet him tonight at dinner; he insisted I join him for dinner for the rest of the voyage. 'Please to accept my most sincere condolences,' he said, and suggested he could arrange for an unscheduled stop on one of the islands to enable me to take Richard off the boat and fly home.

'Absolutely not,' I said. 'I've been looking forward to this cruise all my life and I'm not going to be cheated out of it now. Richard would have wanted it this way.' He would have too, she interjected to me. 'I intend calling my son in America and asking him to join me, if he's able to.' And thank goodness you were, dear.

'He will take Richard's place. If you'll be kind enough to put an extra bed in my suite,' I said, 'my son and I will continue the cruise together.'

'It will be my pleasure,' he said.

"Well, I wasn't going to allow all that money to go to waste. This cruise cost Richard a fortune. Of course all the passengers have been most sympathetic. But I've noticed since you've come on board, dear, one or two of them have been giving me disapproving looks. I think they want me to go home and grieve all over the place, but I'm not doing that, that's not me at all."

This was news to me.

"I want to savour it all and go on," she continued. "Life is for living. We can bury him later when we get back home. We have another ten days of life on the ocean wave, and I'm jolly well going to enjoy it. Meanwhile, Richard's in the fridge downstairs. He won't mind, he'll keep."

And we did have a jolly good time. We went to Grand Cayman and visited a turtle farm, where Vi squealed with delight to be given a twelve-inch baby turtle to hold... in white gloves, Vi, I mean, not the baby turtle. I climbed the great Dunn's River Falls at Ocho Rios while Mother watched and took photographs. We visited Noel Coward's home, 'Firefly', his six-bed roomed house, 1,000 feet above sea level, commanding, as he might have said, 'ravishing views'.

Our bright new alliance was most promising. Though I admit, I did feel a trifle ambivalent about it, the protective shield I'd built around myself would take more than a sea voyage to tear down. I still couldn't come clean about my experiences in Canada. That would not have gone down at all well. The news that I had become gay would have cast a very dark shadow indeed, a shadow that Richard's death, somehow managed to avoid. For she had convinced me her story was true. No, I thought, she couldn't possibly have had a hand in his death, not possibly. Could she?

Chapter Twenty-Four

Petra

1978-01

Changing my life was daunting. Everything that had been cosy and comfortable before was now turned upside down. My marital home was sold for a good price, but I had to give half the money to Annie, so I rented an apartment in Notting Hill while doing the play at the Old Vic and spent my days house-hunting.

I visited a shrink, a wise old witch who lived in Maida Vale who helped me start looking at things differently, solo. I owe her the most enormous debt, for gradually the pain of coals burning in my breast faded and reassembling my life started to be more interesting and even fun. In our talks she asked about my parents. "No," I answered, "Let's only deal with my marriage break-up and change of sexuality, that's quite enough, surely?" The truth was that the development of these two Gordian problems had diminished my tired old botheration of whether Mother was, or wasn't, a killer. I had enough to worry about setting myself in order.

Eventually I found a run-down three-bedroom Victorian house in West London, which I renovated from basement to attic promising myself that my new home would reflect the fresh new me, that everything in it would be chosen with an eye to expressing my shiny new personality – which, of course, was exactly the same as the old one except that now I knew myself slightly better. My divorce became finalised and I managed to see my children on a fairly regular basis. Things were better between us, but not ideal, for they were still both living with Annie's boyfriend. Rebecca, for some reason that I never fathomed out, took her mother's side against me and even changed her surname to that of her mother's maiden name.

In the course of publicising my play, I was interviewed by a smirking lady journalist who asked knowingly, "And are you enjoying your new bachelor life?"

I gave her some bland answer, but realised it might not be long before some scurrilous newspaper discovered my new lifestyle and ran an exposé (this was in 1979, twenty-six years before the civil partnership laws were passed), for I was not exactly keeping a low profile. Nearly every night I was going out to 'Heaven', the gay nightclub under the arches at Charing Cross. Thinking that I'd rather tell Rebecca and James about my change of sexuality myself, than have them read about it in some Sunday tabloid, I took them out to lunch.

I waited till we got to the pudding. "Darlings," I said, "I have something rather important to tell you. I am now gay."

Rebecca and James looked at each other and grinned.

"Dadda, darling," said Rebecca, who was now a feisty fifteen-year old with ambitions to be an artist. "As you brought us up on old Joan Crawford, Bette Davis and Judy Garland movies, this hardly comes as a big surprise."

We hooted with laugher and hugged. They took it so well, I never worried they were embarrassed or censorious in any way. "Well," as Rebecca said, "You brought us up."

I was offered a Middle Eastern tour of a Noel Coward revue called *Oh Coward* – the title was a pun on the successful *Oh Calcutta* – it was backed by British Airways and Hilton International so it would entail staying in grand hotels and be first-class travel all the way – how could I possibly say no? It turned out to be the trip of a lifetime.

The cast was small and delightful. I found myself singing 'Mad Dogs and Englishmen' in Hong Kong, where 'They strike a gong and fire off a noonday gun'; in the Malay states where 'There are hats like plates which the Britishers don't wear'; and where 'In Bangkok at twelve o'clock they foam at the mouth and run.' I sang "Don't Put Your Daughter on the Stage,' to Mrs Worthington in Bahrain, 'Men About Town' to expats in Dubai and 'Don't Let's be Beastly to the Germans' rather inappropriately to Arabs in Amman. I met Prime Ministers and a King – "You have to keep the right side of him. People have been known to disappear," whispered a bejewelled expat to me over cocktails on a yacht in the Gulf of Oman. I cruised on a private schooner around the South China Seas with a Malaysian millionaire who had the hots for me – to whom I tactfully managed a 'Thank you, but no thank you very much'. In Jordan I strolled down what had once been the columned High Street of the ancient city of Jerash, but it was in the rose-red city of Petra that I had my own private epiphany.

Nothing had quite prepared me for Petra, not even Annie's tales of seeing it as a child with her father. I caught an early morning coach from Amman and arrived at Petra at midday. "The giant mountains and vast mausoleums of a departed race have nothing in common with modern civilization, and ask nothing of it except to be appreciated at their true value as one of the greatest wonders ever wrought by Nature and Man." So wrote the 19th century British cleric Dean Burgen on discovering it and that describes how I felt, too.

Wearing khaki shorts, stout shoes and carrying my haversack with a bottle of water, my guidebook and an apple, I set off down the Sik, which was an experience in itself. The Sik is a narrow gorge about a kilometre long leading to the city; it is flanked on either side by soaring high cliffs containing dazzling formations of rock and colour. Reaching the end I had my first glimpse of the Khazneh (the Treasury), a massive facade carved out of dusty pink rock, dwarfing everything around it. It was carved in the first century as the tomb of a Nabataean king, proving the engineering genius of those ancient people. Totally awe-inspiring, it features briefly in the finale of the film *Indiana Jones and the Last Crusade*. There were only a couple of other tourists about, a camel with his Bedouin keeper and two horses. I took photographs and wandered about the hundreds of elaborate rock-cut tombs. As I entered the Petra valley, where, as promised in the guidebook, I was 'overwhelmed by the natural beauty of the place', I discovered I was being followed by a small group of Arab boys. I gave them biros and tubes of Polo mints that I'd learned to carry about me for such a purpose, and when I sat down on a rock to drink and snack on my apple, they gathered around bombarding me with questions. Where was I from? What was life like in England? Tell us about London? What films had I seen? Then the sixty-four-dollar question, "What is A.I.Ds and how do you catch it?" I sensed I had to answer them carefully.

I'd heard the dreadful story of how in Nigeria, condoms had been distributed to the natives who didn't know how to use them, they'd simply blown them up like balloons. Instructions had to be printed, which the authorities had then stapled on to the thousands of condom packets, thus puncturing them and rendering them useless.

Commencing my tutorial, I said, "It is a deadly disease you can catch through having sex..."

"But only sex with men," they laughed knowingly.

"No," I answered sternly. "Sex with anyone. You must never, never mix blood with semen."

"What's semen?"

Oh dear, I thought, are they having me on? "Spunk," I replied. That word they knew. To see their beautiful yet not-so-innocent dirty, downy faces hooting with glee made me smile, and I wondered what would become of them all.

I had arranged to stay overnight in a hostel, sleeping in a dormitory with other tourists, but I was so excited I couldn't sleep. In the middle of the night I got up, dressed and walked down the Sik again.

A silver moonlit sheen shone over everything. The night air was icy but invigorating, sharpening my senses. The silence was uncanny; I could hear nothing but the beating of my heart. The eerie light on the massive rocks endowed them with even more mystery and potency; I walked on a little until I was able to climb onto a ledge. There I lay on a slab of rock staring up at the stars marvelling at space and eternity. Lying on that rock, still warm from the heat of the sun, my thoughts lifted to a spiritual level. These rocks have stood here since the beginning of time, I thought. Since Petra was first established, six centuries before Christ was born. Since Marco Polo linked the spice and silk-trade routes from China and India to Venice and Rome. Since the Crusaders, since Napoleon, since the First World War, since the Second... what were my little problems of a broken marriage compared to them? As nothing. Since I'd not topped myself, surely my life must be worth living? Rise above your troubles, Billy. You're not here long. Through my thin shirt I felt the heat of the rock on my back pulsating strength into me. I extended my arms, my right hand curled round a stone. Extraordinarily it fitted my hand perfectly, miraculously; it seemed to have been wrought by nature especially for me. I lifted it. There were indentations for my thumb and fingers and it made me feel chosen, special. I put it in my pocket. I have it now on my desk as I write. To me it symbolises my growth, a kind of talisman of coherence after years of muddle.

While I was lying there having these philosophical thoughts I heard a voice singing. At first I thought it was a Muslim prayer echoing around the rocks. But then I recognised the song; oddly it was, "I left my heart in San Francisco", and the tenor voice sounded as if it was coming from nearby. To hear this delightful but totally inappropriate song sung in such an other-worldly place at such an hour of the night was bizarre and strangely intriguing. I stood up and walked toward the sound. I rounded a corner and saw a young man sitting cross-legged before an open fire totally wrapped up in himself crooning to an imaginary audience. Amused, I waited till he'd finished his song, and then applauded.

"Bloody Hell!" he yelped, scrambling to his feet.

"Hi there!" I called.

Staring at me he said, "You scared the living daylights out of me."

"Sorry," I said approaching him, "but I don't think you will find it here."

"What's that?"

"Your heart." Grinning, I came nearer, warming my hands by his fire. "What on earth are you doing singing it here at this time of night?"

"Practising. I'm a singer."

"Ah." Lord, I thought, another performer. "It sounded so strange. I mean to hear it now, in this place, but it sounded good, too."

"Thanks. I'm supposed to be doing a gig in Amman next week. My Dad works there and I'm singing it for him really. It's not my kind of thing. I'm more into E. L.O. and the Beatles. Who are you anyway?"

I told him, and we introduced ourselves. He told me his name was Sandy Lane. When I raised a cynical eyebrow, he explained it was his stage name, which he preferred to Costas, his Greek birth name. He was an attractive fellow of about twenty-seven or so with a shock of black hair, wearing a bright red zipped top with yellow stars on it which gave him an air of the circus. I offered him a cigarette and we sat smoking, staring into his fire chatting. I showed him the stone I'd just found and we talked of Time, God, and Fate, heavy subjects, but at the time, in such a setting, they seemed wholly appropriate. As sometimes happens between strangers we told each other our life stories. He said he'd just missed being signed up by E.M.I. Records, and had come out to Jordon to stay with his Father. His mother, he told me, had just died, and he remarked how lucky I was that mine was still with me. I told him one of my Mother tales and in return he told me an amusing family story of his own.

At his parents' wedding, his English grandmother had paid for the hire of the hall. She had been surprised to see her new Greek daughter-in-law in her wedding dress covered, in the tradition of Greek weddings, with gifts of paper money. On stretching out to take a £50 note as pay back, she had her hand severely walloped by the bride's mother, Sandy's Greek grandmother.

We exchanged phone numbers and parted just as an orange dawn was rising. As I walked away I wondered if I'd ever see him again, I rather hoped I would.

It was June when I arrived back home in London after the tour. Within a week I received a phone call from my Aunt Evelyn. Mother, who was then aged seventy-one, had been diagnosed with cancer.

Chapter Twenty-Five

Sorting Underwear

1981–1982

"As you can imagine she's in the most frightful state, Billy," Evelyn told me on the phone. "She won't admit it to anyone. You really should go and see her."

"Of course," I answered. "I'm due to start a new seven-part series for the Beeb next week. We're filming it in Exmouth over the next three months, but I'll try to pop down to see her before I leave, probably this weekend, on Friday."

Wow, I thought as I put down the receiver. I wasn't sad. I wasn't glad. One thing I did know, I knew I'd have to be with her when the end came...if only to ask her why she'd suffocated father all those years ago, and if she really did polish off her next three husbands and Maud. I wasn't going to allow her to go to her death and not tell me that. Standing there with my hand on the receiver, I remembered when I was a kid and had overheard her on the phone hearing the news that a friend of hers had died of cancer. "Oh no," she'd cried. "It's too ghastly. I'll never be able to go to the funeral." Immediately she put down the receiver she went straight to her bedroom to fix a veil onto an old black hat.

At midday the following Friday I rang the front-door bell of Mother's mansion house apartment in Folkstone. A stranger answered the door. She was an over made-up lady wearing a bright red twin set and pearls who asked me in a forthright fashion, "Are you the son?"

"Yes."

"You'd better come in. We thought you were the doctor. She's not at all well. I must say I think you might have made arrangements for someone to be with her. I can't do everything. I've only popped down for a moment. My husband's not well either. I live upstairs."

"Oh! I'm sorry," I said, wondering if I should have organised help. Was that my responsibility? As I opened the living room door Mother was sitting in a house coat with her feet up in front of the electric glow-coal fire, her hair, now quite silver, was coiffed to perfection; she stretched out her arms to me. "My son has come to see me at last," she declaimed dramatically. As I bent to kiss her she gasped in my ear, "Thank God you've come, dear!"

The neighbour woman said, "I must get back to my Frank, Vi."

"You do that," said Mother. "Give him my regards. Now my son is here, I'll be fine. Thank you so much."

The woman went and Mother and I were alone. "She's such a dear," she said. "Jewish, of course."

Not wishing to be drawn on her observation, be it negative or positive, I evasively looked around the room. "The flat's looking nice."

This was only the second time I'd been here. She'd rearranged the furniture and it looked more homely, there were flowers, still no books, but now the room was full of faces, faces of family and friends, all, as I soon realised, faces of the departed. Framed photographs of them, along with ornaments and knick-knacks were strewn everywhere. They stood on the window sills and mantelpiece; on the bureau was her younger brother Cecil, the one whose grave she'd fallen into, but in pride of place hanging over the fireplace were a pair of oval framed pen portraits of her mother – 'Remember Violet, money is like a force of nature. With it you have freedom, without it, you're nothing' – and her adored father.

"He was such a strong, hard-working man," she'd once told me. "He died before I knew him well, but to this day I remember his advice when I was a young girl: 'A woman who has too many men around her, is not considered very nice.' So," she added, with a sigh, "what he'd have made of me, I dread to think!"

Across the hall, her bedroom was a regular portrait gallery of her expired lovers. There was William Dancy, the man she'd told me I'd been named after. There was Joe, dear Joe, whom she'd never loved, but who'd saved her from loneliness, and Richard, husband No 4, who'd actually expired proving his love. Significantly, there was no portrait of my father, or of Stan, but since his fall from grace – the discovery of him fathering an illegitimate daughter – his name was never mentioned. My own image was a framed postcard which hung in the corner, but at least I was there, and flattered to be included in such esteemed company. I think mine was the only portrait of a living person. There were even group pictures of the airmen and soldier boys from the war years at 'The Green Dragon' pub in Croydon. Mother may have outlived them, but she remembered them all and how they had loved her.

In the living room I sat beside her and took her hand. "Mother," I said. "Evelyn's told me everything. Why on earth didn't you tell me?"

"You never rang me," she said defensively. "How could I?"

"The phone works two ways, Mother. You could have called me."

"It's your place to ring me. A son should call his mother every week. Anyway I did call. But I'm not leaving messages with those...those... people you have up there." Her tone implied my 'people' were the very dregs of society.

"What 'people', Mother? That's an answering machine."

"You know perfectly well who I mean. Anyway, I'm not conversing with a wretched machine at my time of life."

"You have to come to terms with modern technology, Mother."

"Oh no, I don't."

I wasn't sure if she was being deliberately stupid or if she was dissembling. I suspected the latter, that she'd spoken to a guest who'd answered my phone, disapproved, and was curious to know who he was and who was now in my life. No doubt she suspected some romantic liaison, and she would have been right, but I, as sure as hell, was not going to volunteer the information.

The door bell rang and I let in the doctor, who disappeared with Mother into her bedroom. After a while she called me in. "I want you to hear this," she said, holding out her hand. I clasped it and she drew me to her side as she lay on the bed.

"Now, as you were saying Doctor. Do please continue."

Dr Ferris was a pleasant grey-haired patrician, the ideal type of conservative gentleman to deliver solemn news. He looked at me as if hesitating.

"It's alright. My son will take care of me," she said, which surprised me. "Tell me truthfully, how long have I got?"

He patted her arm thoughtfully, glanced at me, and sat down on the end of the bed. "You'll be alright for a month or two, but if you insist on refusing chemotherapy, you're going to be in a lot of pain. We can help with that, of course, but then it's going to be quick, anything from three to five months."

Mother's eyes dropped to the coverlet.

I waited, not knowing what to say.

"So," she murmured lightly, a smile hovering round her lips, "I needn't bother with Christmas cards this year then."

Dr Ferris looked urbanely at his clasped hands. "I'll be dropping by to see you regularly."

It was only after he left that she started to cry. She gripped my hand again.

"Billy, I want you to promise me something."

"What's that, Mother?"

"I want you to promise me you'll never put me in a Nursing Home or hospital. I couldn't bear it. I want to die here in my own bed. You understand? You will promise me that, won't you, Billy?"

"Yes, Mother."

"Promise me?"

"I promise."

"Good." She released my hand and started talking very quickly. "Now then, I've been thinking. In the top draw of my chest of drawers over there I keep all my lingerie. I want Rebecca to have it. Open it out and bring it here on the bed. We'll sort it out. There's some beautiful silk and satin underskirts, negligees, all sorts. Little girls love that kind of thing."

Not my little girl, I thought, but I did as she bade me, withdrew the drawer from the chest and with a sinking heart brought it to the bed.

"Empty it all here," she ordered, patting the eiderdown.

I did so, and the next gruesome twenty minutes were spent going meticulously through her underwear: briefs, bras, night-dresses, old Broderie Anglaise petticoats, even 1950s corselettes, to see if they passed muster. Eventually I carried all the so-called good stuff in a bin liner to the boot of my car. Later on, when I passed it to Rebecca, who'd decided by then not to be an artist but an actress (God help her), she came out with, "I'm not wearing any of that old bag's knickers." So Mother's undies ended up at Oxfam.

When I returned from the car, Mother was in the kitchen. I asked about her medication and how often the doctor visited. Mindful of my promise, I thought I'd better arrange some nursing help, so I hit the phones. I called the doctor's surgery, the Social

Services, Macmillan Nurses and Marie Curie Nurses, and then visited their local offices. I was able to organise morning and afternoon visits and for not too much money.

Saturday morning was bright and sunny. Walking with her on my arm down to the local shops we stopped for her to have a rest on a bench by the post box. As people passed I became aware they were recognising me. One couple stopped and asked, "Are you 'Old Roly' from off telly?" My soap from six years ago was being repeated on some television channel so it was like the old days when I went out. After ten minutes or so there was a small crowd asking questions and wanting autographs. Normally I would have fled, but I was getting such a kick out of watching Mother's reaction. A beatific smile had appeared on her face, she positively glowed, her grasp on my arm tightened possessively. She was literally basking in my reflected glory. A lady said to me, "You have given me great joy with your work," then turning to Mother said, "You must be very proud of your son."

"I am," she said.

That gave me great joy.

I returned to London the next day feeling I'd done as much as I could and promised her I'd visit again when I'd finished filming my new telly series.

Three months later, feeling pretty exhausted after completing my contract I rang her front-door bell again.

This time one of the Marie Curie nurses answered the door. "Oh, it's you. The actor. Well," she said with a wry smile, "we all know where you get it from!"

I realised at once Mother had been playing them up.

One does not change character with the knowledge of certain death, I discovered, at least Mother didn't. In fact she became worse. More monstrous, more charming, more demanding, knowing no one was going to disallow her. She was coming up to her best scene, her finale, and, by George, it was going to be a humdinger.

Chapter Twenty-Six

Moving In

1982

"She has a gentleman with her at the moment," said the nurse shutting the front door behind me, she wasn't wearing a nurse's uniform but had a Marie Curie badge on the lapel of her cardigan.

I made my way to the spare bedroom, passing Mother's closed bedroom door. As I set my bag down I wondered how long I should be staying here, for I knew I'd have to see her out. Last month, banking on what Dr Ferris had told us – that Mother would not be around by Christmas – I'd booked a holiday on the island of Tenerife. The flight left Heathrow on 19th December; it was now October 15th.

After a while Mother's gentleman caller left and I went in to see her. She was sitting up in bed wearing a pretty pink bed jacket. As she looked up at me she snapped her handbag shut. She'd lost a great deal of weight and there was a wildness in her eye that was strangely disconcerting. "Such a dear man," she said, tucking her handbag away under the pillow. "He's just repaired the grand-mother clock in the hall and came to return it. People are so kind. How are you, dear? "

"I'm fine," I said, greeting her with a kiss. "What about you?"

"Don't ask. I'm dying," she answered, suddenly assuming a Camille languor. "They're coming from all over to say goodbye to me, the townsfolk."

The phone rang on her bedside table. Immediately she picked it up and I guessed she was in for a chat session so I went to the kitchen to make myself a cup of tea and talk to the nurse, a pleasant plump woman of about thirty. "How is she?" I asked.

"She's certainly enjoying the attention. She'll be glad you're here; she never stops talking about you. Was she ever on the stage too?"

"No," I answered grinning.

"She seems to be a very popular lady. She has lots of visitors."

I wondered about that, reminding myself that no one knew her quite as I did. Later that afternoon she had three more callers; her hairdresser, another middle-aged man, and a young woman who worked at the local supermarket. Into Mother's bedroom they trooped closing the door behind them.

The following morning there were callers every half hour.

I realised she'd once run a pub and knew a lot of people, but that was over twenty years ago and in Canterbury, not Folkestone. What exactly was going on? It took me a couple of days to work it out.

The next morning the postman delivered a registered parcel for her, it was the size of a large cigarette packet and sealed with red wax on the knots; I signed for it and took it in to her.

"Scissors!" she demanded from her bed. "There're in the drawer over there."

I gave her the scissors and watched with interest as she attacked the box with her steel, savagely slicing at the string and brown paper. Eventually a small cardboard box was revealed. Inside it, nestling in white tissue paper were six twinkling eternity rings. She emptied the contents on the eiderdown. Out fell a gleaming white diamond ring, a shimmering deep blue sapphire, a glowing red ruby, a glittering green turquoise, an alternate opal-and-diamond ring, and a knotted-design yellow diamond eternity...and fluttering to the floor, a folded bill.

Deftly, swiftly, Mother removed most of the rings she was wearing and crammed the new ones onto her fingers. They all fitted perfectly. Every finger was now covered in glittering jewelled bands. "Oh," she gasped, spreading out her hands. "Don't they look lovely?"

Indeed they looked superb, extraordinary. Her perfectly-painted scarlet nails, somehow incongruous growing out of such old and bent fingers, now overlaid with rings.

"Very exclusive knuckledusters, Mother," I commented. "Where did they come from?"

"I ordered them from Dennis, my jeweller up in town. He knows my size. I just don't care anymore. Don't they look lovely?" Sensuously she adjusted them.

I could see her point. Wryly I picked up Dennis's account. Actually it wasn't the jeweller's bill; it was his receipt for the six thousand, eight hundred pounds that Mother had already paid.

"Close the door," she ordered. "I don't want that nurse to know everything that goes on."

I shut the door.

"Under the bed is my jewel box," she said in hushed tones. "Fetch it out, will you."

I got onto my hands and knees and looked. There indeed was Mother's handsome white leather jewel case; I pulled it out and placed it on her lap.

She opened the lid. I was staggered at the sight of such a treasure trove. Brooches, strings of pearls, rings and bracelets gleamed. She returned the rings she'd just removed and picked out various pieces showing me which jewels she wished me to pass on to Rebecca and which to my cousins. "But after I've gone, mind," she warned with a smile. "I've written it all down in my Will. Richard has it, Richard Davies, my solicitor, he knows everything."

Returning the box under the bed, I saw something else. "What's this holdall doing?"

"That's where I keep my cash."

I yanked at it and unzipped the top. It was stuffed full of ten and twenty-pound notes, several thousand pounds worth, I judged.

"Whatever have you got all this here for?"

"I use it to pay the tradesmen and people who call."

"What?"

"Well, I like to give them a little something for coming to see me."

No wonder she was so popular. The word had obviously got around; the 'townsfolk' were coming in for their perks.

"The nurses, too," she said. "Well, they get paid so little."

"No, Mother. You don't have to pay the nurses, I've organised all of that."

At first I was angry and contemptuous of her buying her popularity, but then I relented. Vanity, it seems to me, is the most ineradicable of the passions that assail us, being a part of every virtue we may possess. Of courage, certainly of ambition – any artist who desires the limelight must possess some – of love, even the humility of the saint. So be merciful, I thought, let it go. I was more concerned about all that money leaving her account. There wasn't going to be much left for me at this rate. So I telephoned the aforementioned Mr Richard Davies, Mother's lawyer and explained. He understood completely and suggested I take out a Power of Attorney. He arrived the following afternoon with his secretary, and by Mother's bedside it was all arranged. To my relief she was delighted, regal almost, holding a levée in her pink bed jacket. After she signed the document, I said: "Now, Mother, if anyone asks you about money, refer them to me." I removed the holdall from under her bed to a cupboard in my bedroom.

"Thank you, darling," she said. "It's such a relief not to have to worry. Give Richard a whisky, will you. Use one of those crystal glasses, he loves those. I'll have one too." And she did.

To be a compliant visitor at creeping death is not very amusing; however even I had underestimated Mother's star quality, every day she made me smile. It wasn't that I was vindictive or pitiless; I was without emotion, performing, as I saw it, my duty, and thank God there was morphine, so she was never in much pain.

There was a daily happening which I will attempt to describe. Sitting up in bed, leaning on her pillows, she'd place her fingers on her temples. Pushing her hands back slowly, her fingers on her scalp, she forced the loose skin from her eyes and cheeks up, pulling her silvery hair up till it stood on end like a mad woman. Holding her wrinkled arms high, her eyes heavenward, like a ballerina doing a bourrée, she maintained the pose; then, suddenly, let everything fall....arms collapsed, head lolled, eyes shut, inert...death-like.

The first time I witnessed this wondrous display I really thought she'd gone. But after a long wait, she gasped in air, pursed her lips, furious that her end was not yet nigh, shut her eyes again and forced herself dead. Among the nurses this event became known as her 'Dying Swan act'.

"I bet she was a terror," said one of them as I was showing her out one Friday evening. "You can always tell what they were like at this stage. I'm not due back again till next Tuesday, but somehow I don't think I'll be seeing you again. I wish you all the best."

But next Tuesday the nurse returned and life went on...and on, and on. Nurses, night nurses, neighbours, and every visitor that arrived was spellbound by Mother's... I'm tempted to say performance, yet that would imply an act. I came to realise that it wasn't an act. It was simply Mother enjoying the attention, holding the central star role and playing it like a true leading lady. A role nature was reluctant for her to relinquish.

The order of the day was medicine, morphine every four hours, small meals, bedpans when she couldn't make the loo, sorting through clothes with orders to who they were to go to, and towards the end there was holding hands.

"I'd like some nice music," she said, during one such session.

I went to the living room to look through her tapes by the record player. An Irish nurse was sitting smoking. "I saw the ashtray," she said, apologetically holding up her stub. "You don't mind, do you?"

"Of course not," I answered.

"It's a terrible time for you, so it is."

I turned away, thinking, No, it isn't really, and opened up Mother's music centre.

"Anything I can do?" she asked.

"Not at the moment, thanks. I'm trying to find her some music." Inside were all her favourites, Harry Roy, the dreaded Charlie Kunz – 'what I wouldn't give if you could play the piano like Charlie Kunz' – Russ Conway and Liberace. I judged none of these suitable for her present mood so choose one of my earlier birthday presents to her; Julius Katchen's recording of Rachmaninoff's Second Piano Concerto, and took it in to her.

"Ah, *Brief Encounter*," she sighed in a gooey way.

After a slight altercation as to how the tape recorder worked, she listened rapt. In the pause after the first movement she said, "It's so lovely I could eat it," which I thought as good a description of that particular piece of music as you'll find outside of a music critic.

I can't remember if it was later that evening or the next that she gave me the cue I'd long been waiting for. She asked me to plump up her pillows and leant forward to allow me to do so. I plumped the bolster, then two more pillows; just as I was holding up the last one, she deliberately lay back. Looking at me with glinting eyes, she said, "Do it well."

I understood immediately what she meant.

It would be easy. She wanted to go. I wanted her to go. My childhood nightmare of trying to kill her with a floppy stage dagger flashed through my mind. Did I have the courage to help her go now? My fingers tightened around the pillow...soft feathers, squashy, it was my dream made too real.

"Do it well, Billy," she repeated, her eyes shining with excitement. "Put it over my head."

I held my breath. "Like you did to my Father."

Her eyes, like blowtorches, blazed into me. "What?"

"I was under the bed."

She stared at me for a long time without moving. God knows what was going through her medicated drug-fuelled mind. Thinking back fifty years, trying to figure it out... "But..."

"The Headmaster had sent me home for the Armistice."

"You were under the bed? But... You knew? All these years, you've known?"

I nodded. "Why did you do it?"

Very slowly, very deliberately, she answered me. "For the same reason I'm asking you to do it now."

Motionless I stared back at her. How many years had I wanted to kill her? Now she was asking me... pleading. I could actually do it. I had her permission. No one would ever know. I could get away with it. The nurse reading in the living room across the hall was behind two closed doors. Everyone was expecting her to die...any day. Yes. I'd be doing her a favour. Slowly I lowered the pillow.

"Lift your head, darling," I said placing the pillow under her neck. "There. Comfy?"

Chapter Twenty-Seven

Chickens Come Home

1982

I'd let the moment go. I had to be alone. I left her bedroom and went into my own next door. My hands were trembling. I'd not been able to do it. Yet she'd confessed, actually admitted to killing him. I fumbled in my briefcase for a cigarette. I'd stopped smoking months ago but still kept a packet for emergencies. I lit up and exhaled. I opened my bathroom door and stared at myself in the mirror – it threw my face back, taut and white. It would have been easy, so easy. Yet I'd not been able to do it. Was it ethics that had stopped me...or...did I...? God forbid, did I love her? Oh Lord! Don't say that, no. Yet I'd not been able to go through with it. All these years I've known she had blood on her hands, known she had to be punished, yet... though God knows the poor woman is being punished now. She actually excused herself on the grounds of mercy killing, euthanasia, as she just now pleaded with me to do the same to her. That's how she's been able to live with herself all these years. She had no guilty conscience. It would have tormented me, but she's slammed the bolt on the door of her past and forgotten. And what about the others, Maud, Stan, Joe, and Richard? Had she really had a hand in their deaths, too? Annihilating them hadn't been euthanasia; their convenient disappearances were the result of sheer greed, for she'd profited by every single one of their deaths. I had to know what she'd say about that. I damned well was going to ask. She wants to confess, she needs to confess. As I opened my bedroom door, across the hall I saw the nurse in the kitchen preparing a meal.

"I'll be off once she's eaten this," she said glancing over to me. But as she caught sight of my expression she hesitated, "Are you alright, sir?"

"Fine," I answered, making an effort to look it.

"It's a stressful time for you. You should get away for a bit."

"Funny you should say that. I've booked a holiday for Christmas, but keep wondering if I should cancel it."

She picked up the tray and looked at me. "I wouldn't do that, Mr Bartlett. I don't think she'll be here by then," and she took Mother's broth into her.

After the nurse had left for the day, Mother asked to go to the lavatory. I suggested she use the bedpan, but no, she insisted that I should take her to the toilet. Was some perverse streak in her testing me? As I helped her on and off the loo, all her queenly dignity abandoned, awareness of the full circle of life was not uppermost in my thoughts, but sitting at her bedside afterwards it did occur to me. How often, I wondered had she done that for me when I was a child? I'd been just a baby when she'd had her breakdown and sent me away. I was seven when she'd brought me home, when I re-joined her and Stan at Selsey Bill and she asked me to call him 'Daddy'.

"What time is it?" she asked.

"Twenty to four," I answered.

"I'm going at four," she announced.

After the night nurse had arrived, she lay back and asked again, "What time is it?"

"Seven o'clock," I said.

"Seven!" she queried. "Seven! I shouldn't be here. Why am I

still here? Why hasn't he taken me? Why doesn't he take me?"

"He knows what a fusspot you are, darling," I joked, resting my hand on her wrist. "He's redecorating for you." She didn't smile but I could feel her pulse racing.

"I shouldn't be here. Why hasn't he taken me? Why?" Frowning, she subsided for a while. Suddenly she shouted at the ceiling, berating God for his tardiness, "Why don't you take me? Take me! Why don't you take me? WHY?"

"Try to relax, Mother," I said as soothingly as I knew how. "Be calm, darling, please."

For a while she appeared to obey and then very quietly said, "I've told such wicked lies, that's why. I've been so wicked. So many wicked things I've done. I've made your life a torment, haven't I?"

I held my breath staring at her. Had she really said that? Had I heard her correctly?

"Haven't I?" she insisted.

Had she known all along how she'd bedevilled and plagued my life? Our entire history, which had known so few moments of tenderness, love or joy, seemed to flash in a moment before me. A part of me wanted to scream at her, "You've known! All these years you've known what you were doing to me," but stroking the back of her hand, I found myself saying, "Don't be silly, Mother. I don't know what you're talking about."

"Forgive me," she persisted. "Promise me you'll forgive me, Billy"

"You're talking rubbish, Mother."

Putting both her hands out to hold mine, she ordered, "Look at me." Her grip was just a memory of the strength she'd once had, but her eyes blazed with their old intensity. "Promise me you'll forgive me? Promise me?"

I looked into those eyes I knew too well, those eyes that had haunted me a lifetime. They were no longer deep aquamarine, but grey, milky almost, begging, imploring, waiting for my answer. But it was far too late for revenge. I think I may have smiled a little as I said: "Of course, Mother. Nothing to forgive."

She lay back exhausted, emaciated, but still clasping my hand. "You come with me, Billy. You come too." Retrieving her hand to place it in prayer, she addressed the Almighty again. "Please, God, take Billy and me together. We'll go together."

"Hold on, Mother! Oh no, we won't. I'll get you to the door, but I won't actually come in, if you don't mind. Not just yet awhile."

"You come with me," she muttered. "You come with me," and she appeared to doze.

"Mother!" I murmured after a while.

"Mmm?"

"When you say you've done wicked things... what did you mean?"

She opened her eyes and looked at me, then they seemed to shift focus onto space. "I made so many mistakes. Wicked I was. Unfaithful to my Bernard."

"With whom?" I ventured, glancing at the photographs of her lovers around the room. "Was it William Dancy?"

"How did you know....?"

Not to betray Evelyn's confidence, I said, "You told me I was named after him."

"Ah yes." She caressed my hand. "When you were born I wasn't sure whose you were...I thought you were his. Wasn't that silly? But you grew up to look just like my beloved Bernard. But then he left me... I couldn't cope on my own, Billy. That's why I sent you away. Why I abandoned you. You do forgive me, don't you?"

"Yes, Mother," I answered, remembering Eve's story.

"But he came back to me in the end. It was me he loved really."

I swallowed hard, determined to press on, to discover the truth. "And what about Maud?"

"Who?"

"Stan's sister, Maud, who left you all her money."

"Ah yes, dear woman. What about her?"

"Did you push her off that mountain?"

A naughty grin slowly filtered up into her face. "Tripped up the bitch, you mean? I should have. Dreadful woman, she was. So jealous, so possessive."

"Of Stan? What about Stan, Mother? And Joe and Richard?"

"What about them, dear?"

"Did you kill them?"

She stared at me for a long time. "Is that what's been bothering you all these years?"

I nodded.

"You are funny. You always did have a vivid imagination. But maybe you needed that for your work." She closed her eyes. "I think I could sleep a bit now."

That night I slept fitfully. I woke and went into her room. The night nurse was sitting reading by a table lamp outside her door in the hall. Mother was asleep but her eyebrows were knitted in a deep frown. Her pulse was irregular but surprisingly strong. I placed my third finger between her brows and smoothed away the frown. I waited a while, watching over her, stroking her hair, which was still thick, silver and wavy, the skull clearly discernable beneath her bony forehead, her perfectly-arched eye sockets. Yes, she had been a beautiful woman. Of course I loved her. How could I ever have thought otherwise?

The next day followed the pattern of the previous ones, except that in the afternoon Mother complained of pain. I asked the nurses – there were two of them by this time – if we could increase the dose of morphine. Recently, when a junior helper had been on duty, she'd asked me to sign for her 'fix' of morphine, but this nurse answered, "Only with the doctor's permission."

I telephoned the surgery for Dr Ferris.

He was unavailable I was told, someone else would be sent. Forty-five minutes later a bank manager arrived. In fact bank managers have more compassion in my experience than the portly toad that turned up to examine Mother, who, by this time, was groaning in agony.

"Yes, well, I can see she's had enough," he said pompously buttoning up his double-breasted pin-striped suit.

"That is an understatement, Doctor. You can see she's in great pain, could you not increase her medication?"

"No, no, quite unethical. Rinse out her mouth, that will make her feel better." He snapped up his bag and left.

I was furious, I realised, of course, that we were in euthanasia territory, nevertheless...

Looking out of the window I noticed it was early evening. The trees were bare, their stark black branches, like spider's legs, were silhouetted against the grey sky, the light was going. I decided. I knew what I had to do.

I looked out her prettiest nightgown and, with the help of the nurse, changed and dressed her. She moaned but still attempted smiles, despite the pain that each movement gave her, grateful for what we were doing. I combed her hair, and she lay back, but her brows frowned in torment. "Stop the pain, Billy. Stop the pain."

"It'll go soon," said the nurse. "We'll just be outside if you want anything," and she left us, leaving the bedroom door wide open.

"It'll go soon," I repeated, shutting the door firmly.

"Grip my hand," said Mother.

I did so.

"Fight me," she ordered. "Fight the pain for me."

I pressed her palm a little.

"Harder," she ordered.

With my fingers entwined in hers I pressed.

With all her strength she tried to push my hand back, but I felt only a little pressure. Gently I took her hand to my lips and kissed it. I tucked both her hands beneath the coverlet and kissed her frowning forehead. "Love you, darling," I said. Picking up the pillow by her side I swiftly covered her face. Pressing hard I waited. There was a long, long silence. Her shoulders suddenly gave a spasm and then seemed to be still. I waited I don't know how long, praying to my long-ignored God that her suffering would cease, that I was doing right thing, the humane thing, that the nurses wouldn't return and discover me. I removed the pillow and felt her pulse. I couldn't find it. Was it all over? I opened the door and called in the nurses. "I think she's gone."

My eyes were dry as I watched them examine her, wondering if they could tell what I'd just done.

One of them turned and gave me a nod. "Blessed relief," she sighed. "I'd better call the doctor back."

Oh no, I thought, not that dreadful bank manager again. He might detect suffocation. Anxiously I waited, but mercifully it was Dr Ferris who arrived. While he was in the bedroom with Mother, I called the Funeral Director from the phone in the hall. As the doctor emerged, he said, "I'm glad you were able to be with her. She always spoke so highly of you. Such a charming lady, I'm only sorry she had to go through so much pain. Here," he handed me a piece of paper, "you'll need this for the Registrar." It was Mother's death certificate.

We shook hands and he left.

I looked down at the piece of paper. As the cause of death he'd written: 'Carcinomatosis'.

Had I got away with it?

While we waited for the funeral director, the nurses helped me remove Mother's rings with the aid of Vaseline; I undid her pearls and the thin gold chain she always wore around her neck, I kissed her for the last time and left her to the undertaker's men, who seemed to arrive within minutes. While the nurses were tidying up in the kitchen, I sat in the hall outside Mother's closed bedroom door stunned by what I'd done, waiting for I knew not what. When the door opened there was a picture I'd not bargained for, the macabre sight of Mother being carried into the hall and out of her front door zipped up in a black plastic bag.

I thanked the two saint-like Marie Curie nurses for all they'd done and they left.

The apartment, so full of the tension of death for the last two months, was empty. I wandered about from room to room not knowing what to do. I couldn't help but feel it was like being in a deserted theatre after the curtain had fallen, when the actors and audience had left. In her desk in the living room was her Deed box, in it her Will and all her papers waiting for me to go through. I knew I'd have to do it eventually, but not just now, not now. I couldn't face it. For something to do, I turned on the television. The Wizard of Oz was playing. The Munchin's were singing 'Ding Dong, the Witch is Dead.' Years ago I would have laughed at the aptness of the song, right now I flinched at how inappropriate it was; biting my lip I angrily snapped it off. My anger, I realised, was directed at my former self for hating her so. Now that I admitted to loving her, now that I'd proved my love by what I'd just done: by shortening her suffering, by helping her over, by killing her, I was appeased, confident it had been an act of mercy, not of hatred. No more hatred. No more Mother.

I spent the evening phoning family and friends. I was now the senior generation and tomorrow I'd have a lot to do.

Chapter Twenty-Eight

Finding the Letter

1982-83

"You've been in and out of this Will like a Jack in the box," said Richard Davies, Mother's solicitor, the document laid out before him on his desk. "Unfortunately," he continued, smiling at me somewhat glumly, "in this her most recent Will, you're out of it."

I sat opposite him in his splendid office facing the English Channel, not quite taking it in. "I beg your pardon?"

"Her entire estate," he went on, leafing through the pages, "is bequeathed to her niece, Mrs Elizabeth Cooper. I have an address here for her in Florida."

I shut my eyes in disgust. To make matters more frustrating, in my hand I held an earlier Will, I'd found this morning in her desk, naming me, in the event of her husband Stanley predeceasing her, as her beneficiary; but it was dated 1956. I could hear her voice when I'd refused to drive her home from Joe's cottage but offered to pay for a taxi: "Oh, you'll pay, I'll see to that", and in the Clifton Hotel, Folkestone in 1977: "You'll get nothing from me when I trade in my clogs." So, here we were, sans clogs, and sans birthright. Why, then, was I so surprised? I suppose because since she'd said that, our relationship had undergone such a roller coaster of emotions, I'd forgotten.

"Regarding the Power of Attorney we arranged last month," concluded Mr Davies, "that, of course, now becomes void." He rose from his chair indicating our interview was over and shook my hand. "I am so sorry about this, but," he shrugged, "my hands are tied. There's nothing further I can do."

Standing in the street outside his office, I cursed her. What a cow! After all these years when I finally come around to admitting that I love her, the bitch goes and does this. Well, at least no one can accuse me of killing her for her money.

My next call was to the Registrar's office to report her death. Then I returned to her apartment and her desk.

The middle drawer was stuffed with her old diaries; mostly small handbag-sized, and a few larger ones. How far did they go back, I wondered? How many secrets were buried here? I leafed through one, dated 1942. There were appointments, birthdays and anniversaries; one entry read '10.45. Euston Stn. Pick up Billy with William!!' Those two exclamation marks gave me pause. In view of Eve's story and what Mother had confessed yesterday, that he might have been my father, I understood what they meant. I opened another dated 1966. An entry read: "How is it that no matter how much your children hurt you; you still go on loving them?" It did not make comfortable reading. I had hurt her as she had hurt me. I thought of my own children and how I loved them despite the pain they'd given me when they'd left home to join Annie, when Rebecca had changed her surname to her mother's; that 'full circle of life' thought kicked in again.

I opened the Deed box and emptied the contents out onto Mother's favourite Tabriz carpet. Sitting on the floor I delved into the documents to see if there was anything vital I had to attend to. Here was her birth certificate, 'Born: Aylesbury. 23th March, 1910', some investment bonds and the deeds of the mansion flat, now worth a fortune. After our lifetime of wars it would now all go to my cousin in Florida, along with most of the jewels under the bed. It wasn't the loss of her considerable estate that hurt, it was the rejection, the dumping.

I turned over a yellowing sheet of cardboard. To my amazement and delight it was a ten- by-eight inch mounted studio photograph of my father, Bernard. I'd never seen it before, but though his handsome face had long faded from my memory I knew it was he in an instant. To see him in his prime, aged about twenty-seven in a dark suit and tie looking like a young suave me, gave me a distinct rush of pleasure, but my emotions were saturated in sadness. I sat looking at it fascinated. My eye wandered to the papers scattered before me and suddenly, astonishingly, I noticed a letter addressed to me. I picked it up and looked at it curiously. The postage frank on the envelope was dated 20th December 1937. It wasn't in Mother's handwriting and it had been opened. I took the letter out of its envelope. It was from my father.

The Curzon Hotel. Brighton.

Dear Billy

Thank you very much for your Christmas card, it was very nice and I have it on the mantelpiece in my bedroom. I wish you had written to me before and I would have seen Father Christmas for you and asked him to send you a nice present from Brighton. But here is a lot of money to buy one with, and Mummy will see it is nice.

We may not be able to see each other for a while. When you are older, I hope you will understand why, please remember it has nothing to do with you. I want you to know that whatever happens I love you very much. I am very glad to hear that you are a good boy at school and that you are learning a lot. I have great dreams for your future, and trust that when the day comes that we meet again, we will become firm friends and I will prove a more dutiful father.

Be a good boy at home and be kind to Mummy.

Cheerio, old boy and a very happy Christmas.

All my love.

Daddy.

Tears came to my eyes.

Mother had kept this letter from me for forty-six years.

Among the other documents was a thick envelope. I opened it. It contained all four of her marriage certificates – and, intriguingly, attached to each one with a paper clip was the appropriate husband's death certificate. She'd obviously thought it important that they should be viewed together. Immediately I looked under the cause of death on my father's certificate. It confirmed what she'd told me all those years ago, 'Consumption', the old-fashioned word for tuberculosis.

She'd even included her sister-in-law Maud Hunt's death certificate, whose fatal fall from Striding Edge ridge was recorded as death from: 'Multiple injuries'.

Stan's death from the bee sting was recorded as 'Anaphylactic shock'.

Joe's fall from the apple tree was set down as 'Cerebral thrombosis.'

Richard's, who'd died on the job, was described as 'Myocardial infarction'.

On the front of the envelope she'd written one word, "Absolution", which indicated to me a certain concern that five such close family deaths might give rise to comment, and if so, she needed proof of her innocence.

Perhaps after all she did have something to hide?

Oh no, I thought, don't go there. I must let it rest.

If I'd not witnessed her put Father out of his misery all those years ago, it would never have occurred to me to suspect her of killing anyone. That one fatal, misunderstood act, had disenchanted my childhood and polluted our entire relationship...that and a sprinkling of her off-centre idiosyncrasies, notably her love of funerals. As I contemplated this I became overwhelmed by what might have been, what could have been between us. The influence of the past, or rather my perception of it, had been so great it had warped my judgement of her beyond all repair. Only now, too late, did I see it was false. She had been a woman like any other – well, not quite – who had tried, like women in other lands and other times, to raise herself up from her humble start in life to a respectable position in society and achieve a comfortable old age, and in that, she had succeeded – and that was not nothing.

From my breast pocket I took Mother's death certificate the Registrar had given me earlier with Dr Ferris' description of the cause of death, 'Carcinomatosis', neatly printed, and clipped it next to my Father's death certificate. Those two documents, I concluded, belonged together, for they each gave the lie to the truth, but disguised an abiding, if unlawful, act of love. Which I had to believe in, or I could not continue living with a clear conscience.

I put them in my suitcase, packed my toiletries, picked up Mother's holdall full of cash – that was the least I deserved – locked up the front door and went home, where Sandy Lane, the Pop singer guy I'd met last year in Petra, was waiting for me. Two days later on the 19th of December, as we had planned last October, we flew out of a freezing London into the warm sun of Tenerife for our Christmas holiday.

Finally, about the funeral.

The Funeral Director had assured me that sometimes, while families went to Australia or wherever, he kept the deceased in his chapel for as long as four weeks before burial. I knew he really meant the fridge, but took his point that he wanted to keep his business to a minimum over the Christmas holiday. So the cremation was arranged for the 4th of January.

James had flu that day so I told him to stay in bed, but Rebecca, although she made no secret of the fact that she disliked her grandmother, joined me and stood by me.

I didn't speak, the local vicar, who Mother had never known, took the service, but he had been well-coached by Evelyn. He gave a touching eulogy about how artistic, generous, talented, loved and loving Mother had been. She was truly centre stage; no one upstaged her, and it all went off smoothly. As we stood watching the coffin slide out of sight and the gold curtain slowly closed, that invisible silver cord that replaces the umbilical finally snapped within me and I was unable to stop myself from weeping. Evelyn and I grasped each other's hand, and she said, eyes brimming with tears, "I shall miss my bossy sister."

The sun shone; there was a healthy turn-out and many flowers. At the wake afterwards in one of those large hotels on Folkstone Leas, everyone agreed she'd been a very remarkable woman. Oh yes, I'm perfectly sure Mother would have loved the funeral, if, that is, she could have been persuaded to attend.